HIGHLANDER'S CHRISTMAS

Called by a Highlander

MARIAH STONE

Then came a moment of renaissance,
I looked up – you again are there
A fleeting vision, the quintessence
Of all that's beautiful and rare.
— Alexander Pushkin

PROLOGUE

Carlisle, December 20, 1299

THE WAY THROUGH THE BORDERLANDS TO CARLISLE swarmed with highwaymen, raiders, and thieves. Galloping on the horse through the snow-covered forest, Deidre Maxwell hadn't encountered anyone today, but she wouldn't be safe until she was in the town.

"Faster," she whispered to the horse. The line of granite walls and the donjon of the castle darkened against the leaden sky in front of her. She just needed to cross a white field to reach the town.

She spurred the horse on. Her dagger and the sword she'd stolen from the weaponry swayed on her belt. Not stolen. Borrowed. Her father hadn't taught her sword-fighting against her mother's wish for nothing. She'd never had to use any of her weapons in all the times she'd made this journey alone. It was unusual for a young woman of standing, but she was not a regular lass. She could protect herself, and her family were used to her independent spirit and to her long outings. She'd be all right once she reached the walls.

Her heart drummed against her rib cage. She had such news for Hamish... Such news! God had bestowed happiness upon them, a sign that they should be together.

A small worm of doubt coiled in the pit of her stomach. What if Hamish wasn't as excited as she was? Aye, there would be the issue of persuading her father and mother that they should wed, given that Hamish had no title or land and had grown up on a farm on the Isle of Skye. They'd need to let go of the idea of her marrying Sir Richard Brown. It wouldn't be easy to convince them, but if she and Hamish stuck together, they'd persevere.

Despite the speech she gave herself, she wasn't sure what Hamish would do. He was a wild horse, an untamed stallion who could set her blood ablaze just by looking at her. She'd see him, and her stomach would squeeze in anticipation, as though before a jump into the sea from a cliff.

She rode through the open gates into the town. The guards followed her with their heavy gazes. Aye, she was dressed well and a woman alone, which was unusual, but there was nothing to cause alarm. She huddled deeper into her cloak and pulled the edge of her hood farther down over her forehead. Not that they'd recognize her. It was a town, after all.

Once they were inside the walls, she let the horse walk calmly. She rode on the streets between wooden houses with thatched roofs. Slush mixed with mud slurped under the horse's hooves. The air smelled of woodsmoke and baked goods. People were getting ready for Christmas. Sheep would be slaughtered for pies, geese and chickens for roasts. Pastries would be baked, ale and wine would be drunk. Songs would be sung. Mayhap, she could persuade her father to invite Hamish for Christmas. Hopefully, it would be the first one among many.

She directed the horse to the right and through the heart of town, heading to the outskirts of Carlisle where her maid's sister, Innis, lived with her husband, Simon. The unmistakable, foul scent of Simon's leather tannery told her she'd almost arrived. The hides had to be soaked in urine and pounded with dung. Even Caerlaverock's latrines didn't reek like that, but Hamish had lodged at Simon and Innis's ever since he'd been wounded after protecting the woman from thieves on a dark, empty street. Deidre had to see him, and he was worth enduring a little stink.

The house stood apart from other houses with their broken window shutters, holes in the thatched roofs, and doors that hung askew.

Deidre dismounted and knocked on the door. Loud screams and moans came from the inside. Was Innis finally in labor?

She knocked. The door opened, and Hamish's handsome face appeared in the opening. When he dealt with others, his black eyes were often hard and cold, but when he saw her, they always softened.

"Lass..." He looked back inside the house. The moans grew louder. "Innis is having a bairn."

"Are ye helping?"

"Aye. A wee bit." He brushed her cheek with his big, callused hand, and it sent jolts of sweetness through her skin, making her knees wobbly. He quickly glanced to the left and right, then leaned to her and planted a kiss on her lips that turned her blood to warm honey and made her breasts ache.

"Oh, how I wish to kiss these lips and dinna ever stop."

Deidre took his hand and tugged him after her. "Ye dinna have to stop."

Something dark and sad flickered through his eyes, and a bad feeling stabbed her gut. She chased it away.

"I have something important to tell ye." She pressed out a smile.

"So do I, lass." He looked back into the house. "Simon, will ye manage without me?"

"I thought ye'd never ask," came Innis's voice. "Leave. Simon and the midwife are more than enough."

"First, she begged me to be there, hold her hand. Now she doesna want me." He grabbed his cloak and closed the door behind him. "Come, let's talk."

They rode the horse through the city and headed towards a small, sweet grove with a brook where they'd spent their time together during summer. There was a big, old oak surrounded by thick bushes where Hamish had made love to her for the first time. Aye, what a perfect place to bring him the news.

Hamish dismounted first and caught Deidre as she slid down the beast's back and into his arms. He held her for a moment, his mouth parting in his black, short beard.

God, he was so tall. She wasn't a small lass, but she only reached to his shoulder.

"There isna anywhere safer than yer arms," she whispered, her breath rising in slight puffs of steam with each word.

Again, there was that sadness and hurt in his eyes. "Lass..."

"What is it, Hamish? Did something happen?"

"Nothing's happened, lass." But his voice sounded as though he'd just buried someone. Cold iron clasps began tightening around Deidre's heart. He let her go, and she walked a few steps away, her pulse pounding.

"So what did ye want to say to me?" she said.

He walked towards the brook and stood with his back to her, leaning against a tree with one hand. His shoulders slouched. "'Tis the last time I can see ye, lass."

A knife cut right through her stomach.

"Why?"

He turned to her, and that sadness flickered through his eyes and disappeared.

"Because I stayed for far too long. My last mission ended

moons ago, and yet I'm still here. I stayed for ye. But 'tis time to go."

Every word hit her in the chest, kicking all breath out of her. "Ye dinna wish to marry me then?"

He blinked. "Marry ye?"

"Are ye serious? What about ye bedding me for months?"

He marched towards her and stopped, looming over her. "I didna invite ye to bed me. If ye remember, ye came to me."

A chill ran through her at the steel in his voice. His eyes grew as hard as stone, and as dangerous as a wolf's. There he was—the dangerous predator who wouldn't hesitate to tear his prey apart. Did he look like that when he did the dirty work of rich noblemen? Stealing, blackmailing, spying, threatening.

Killing.

It didn't matter to her. She loved him. She accepted him exactly the way he was.

"Aye, I did," she said. "And why shouldna a woman do what she wants? Why is it only men who may bed women outside of wedlock?"

"I never promised ye a wedlock," he said darkly. "I thought we had an understanding."

"An understanding? And what understanding would that be?"

"That the daughter of the laird of the Maxwell clan wants to have her fun with a cur like me until she weds the right man."

"It doesna matter to me that ye're lowborn, nae one wee bit. I hate that I must marry a man I've never seen in my life. How boring my life would be if all I had was a household to run, cooking and weaving like my mother and my sisters. Nae, I want more."

I want ye, her heart said.

"Aye, I ken ye're nae an ordinary lass. Ye never do things the regular way. But I'm nae the answer to yer rebellion. If ye dinna want to weave and embroider and such, mayhap 'tis best ye join a convent."

Deidre gasped. "A conve— Unbelievable!"

And this was the man she loved? Should she tell him about the bairn at all?

"Look." Hamish walked back towards the brook and kicked a snow-covered hummock into the black, gurgling water. "I've never promised ye anything."

"So ye dinna feel anything for me? Nothing at all?" The words tore at her throat, and her voice rasped.

"'Tis dangerous to feel anything for anyone, lass. Life can take people ye care for so easily from ye. And there's nothing ye can do to change that. 'Tis out of yer control. The only way to keep that control is to be alone. 'Tis my way."

She shook her head. "Well, I wish I'd known this sooner."

Before she'd fallen in love with him. Before she'd given everything to him—her body, her heart, her future.

Only to have him crush it into dust.

"Thank ye for teaching me a valuable lesson, Hamish." She marched towards her horse and mounted. "'Tis the people one cares for who wound the most."

She wouldn't inflict her baby upon the man who didn't want it—or her.

"I hope one day ye ken what a mistake ye just made." She glanced over her shoulder. "Go and live yer lonely life. And I'll live mine."

Only she'd never be alone again. She sent the horse into a hard gallop to get as far away from him as possible. She'd have a sweet bairn to love and protect, and she'd teach them not to trust their heart to another so easily.

But now she had to deal with the consequences of being pregnant out of wedlock. What were her parents going to do once they found out?

CHAPTER 1

Scottish West March, December 20, 1308

HAMISH STIRRED THE POTTAGE IN THE FIELD POT OVER THE campfire, and steam rose from the bubbling liquid. The scent of salted pork, oats, and peas was homey, even in the dead-cold winter forest. With only the few ingredients he had with him, the soup was weak, and he hoped for some proper stew at Innis's house in Carlisle later this evening. He was looking forward to seeing her and her bairns. He hoped the money he'd been sending her since Simon died had kept her from having to sell her body to feed them.

Hamish craved a warm bed. He'd been on the run for a sennight. An assassin sent by John MacDougall had tried to slit his throat but had gotten Hamish's dagger in his heart instead. John MacDougall was the chief of the MacDougall clan, and Hamish's previous employer. MacDougall blamed Hamish for the loss of his arm and his lands to Robert the Bruce after the Battle of the Pass of Brander. In the battle,

Hamish had fought for the English and the MacDougalls, but he'd helped clan Cambel. Despite the fact that one of his missions the year before had been to kill Craig Cambel, he'd grown to like them.

Having John MacDougall as an enemy was bad. Even though MacDougall was currently in England, he still wanted Hamish dead. He needed to hide somewhere the man wouldn't think to look for him. The Borderlands were perfect. With the constant raids and clashes between English and Scots, he could always get lost and find work there. Plenty of people needed a bodyguard, a spy, or a thief.

Hamish huddled deeper into the woolen plaid he had over his *leine croich*, the heavily pleated and quilted war coat he wore. It was freezing cold, but he and his horse needed some rest and a meal before they could continue on to Carlisle. Hamish wanted to be there before nightfall. His path lay through the Maxwell lands in the Scottish West March, and he wanted to pass through them as quickly as possible.

It would be painful, of course, because behind every tree and every bush, he'd see Deidre.

Whenever he had a quiet moment for himself, he thought of her. Now that he was near her lands, memories of her flooded his mind, bringing a dull ache to his heart. Not a day went by that he didn't imagine her icy-blue eyes, her mane of wavy hair the color of aged bronze, and the freckles on her nose that he'd called golden stardust. She was his beautiful, stubborn lass with more fire than a city set ablaze.

Where was she now? Was she happy? Marrit? Did she have bairns of her own? The thought of her with another man slashed his gut like a thousand knives.

A breeze brought the scent of lavender and freshly cut grass. That was odd since they were in the middle of winter. He looked around. Mayhap a merchant was passing by? But no. He was alone in the woods. Everything looked calm among the naked trees shooting into the gray, winter sky. A crow cawed somewhere nearby.

His gaze fell on a faerie circle about ten feet away to his right. It was comprised of three rings of black rocks, the outer circle was three paces broad. He'd noticed it before and chuckled, thinking how peculiar it was to find such a thing. The inner ring was small, and the stones wouldn't even reach his ankle bone, but the layer of snow was thin, so the ring was still rather obvious.

Yes, it was odd, but not enough that he would start believing in faeries. He turned back to his pottage and stirred it. The oats were cooked, and so were the peas, and he decided it was time to eat. He found a bowl in one of his travel sacks.

"Something here smells delicious," said a female voice.

He glanced up and saw a woman standing by the faerie circle. She wore a long dark-green hooded cloak over bright-copper hair that flowed in long waves. She had unusually green eyes that stared at his field cauldron with the curiosity of a cat.

"Delicious?" Hamish chuckled. "A grave exaggeration, I'm afraid. But ye're welcome to have some if ye're hungry."

Her eyes shone, and she came to sit on the log by his side, licking her lips. "Oh, aye. I am hungry."

The scent of lavender and grass intensified as Hamish studied her. Where could it come from in winter? Ah, women. They always found ways to look and smell better. What did he know? Shrugging the strange feeling off, he poured the pottage into the bowl, making sure he scooped more of salted pork and peas for her. He gave her the bowl and the spoon, and she huddled over it. She stirred it, tried the pottage, and coughed. "Hot! Hot!"

"Aye, sorry," Hamish said.

"'Tis all right. Doesna hurt nae more. Are ye nae eating?"

"After ye finish. Ye have my only bowl."

"Oh." She cocked her head, studying him. "Ye're kind, are

ye nae? Rough on the outside, but yer heart is soft." She blew on the spoon and ate some of the pottage.

Hamish chuckled. "Soft heart, ye say? Dinna ken about that. Ye may be more sorry ye ate it than if ye'd gone hungry."

"Nae. It takes a kind soul to feed a complete stranger." She ate another spoonful. "My name is Sìneag, and I have something important to tell ye. The warden of West English March, George Tailor, is looking for a man for a job. Ye look like someone who may be perfect for it."

Hamish narrowed his eyes. "What kind of a job?"

"A dangerous kind. The kind ye'll do well."

Hamish wasn't a stranger to hints and implications. When a powerful man needed someone to be gone quietly, this was how they talked. "All right. And how do ye ken that?"

"I have my ways." She blew on the soup and sipped. "Aye, 'tis good! Mmmmm..." She cocked her head from side to side and even closed her eyes. Hamish cooked well, but not that well. Either she was pretending, or she hadn't had anything to eat for days.

"I need to tell ye something," she said through a mouthful. After she swallowed, she continued. "I have the gift of foresight, and if ye take the job, ye may find more than what ye were looking for. Ye may find yer true love."

Hamish bit his lip, so he didn't burst out in bitter laughter. "Love is a lie, Sìneag, and it only brings pain. I wilna fall into that trap."

He'd learned that lesson early. When he was five years old, a childless couple from the Isle of Skye adopted him after he lost his parents. A year of hard labor passed, and Fiona, a sweet, blond lass the same age as him came to live on the farm as well. While Bearnas and Paedaran beat him daily and worked him like a farm horse, Fiona was the only one who was kind to him. She was often on cooking duty, and she always saved an extra bannock for him, or put an extra ladle of stew in his bowl while Bearnas and Paedaran didn't look.

In the evening, when their adoptive parents were asleep, Hamish and Fiona told each other stories of faeries, of ancient kings, queens, and heroes. The stories distracted them from their miserable existence. They made plans of how they'd escape and find their own farm and marry each other. They would treat their children with kindness and care, not like how Bearnas and Paedaran had treated them.

They were both too young to understand romantic love, but they were devoted to each other in a strange sibling relationship that ran deeper than love.

One day, when Hamish was twelve, Fiona got sick. Hamish begged Bearnas to let the lass rest, but the woman only slapped him and beat Fiona with a stick. She was sure Fiona wanted a day off work, which was unacceptable in the harvest season.

But Fiona got sicker and sicker. She couldn't move. She ran a fever and coughed until her lungs ached. Hamish cared for her, for which he received a heavy beating, but after a couple of days, he woke up next to a still, cold Fiona, her eyes staring into space, and her lips pale.

There was no one else who cared for him, and no one else he cared for. If only Bearnas and Paedaran hadn't been so selfish and cruel. If they'd let her rest, she might be alive now. They'd taken from him the only kin he'd had, the only person he'd loved, and the only future he'd imagined for himself. They'd taken a part of his soul.

Sìneag cocked her eyebrow and hid an amused smile. "We'll see." She handed him his empty bowl and the spoon. "Thank ye for this. I must be on my way, but I wish ye luck with the warden's job, if ye take it."

She stood up and walked away, but Hamish called after her. "Are ye certain 'tis safe for ye to travel alone on foot?"

"Dinna fash, good man. I have my ways."

He watched her move off into the woods, and soon, her green coat disappeared behind the trees. He arrived in Carlisle at twilight and asked the guards for directions to the warden's house, which turned out to be easy to find. It stood across the market square near the church, right in the center of the town. A stone wall surrounded it, and Hamish could see it had two levels, and unlike most houses in the town, it was built of stone.

That made him think of the stone house he wanted to have. Being an assassin and a spy paid well, and he'd been saving coin for years and years now. He only needed a little more before he could settle on an island in the Western Isles. Farmers paid a quarter of a pound per year to rent a cottage, but the MacDonald clan had agreed to let Hamish rent the Isle of Benfar for a single payment of ninety pounds. This would grant him the right to live there undisturbed for the rest of his life. The agreement was unusual, and the sum was exuberant, but the MacDonalds had given Hamish as close to right of ownership as they could. Only the king could actually own, and he bestowed this land to his nobles. Hamish planned to build a house on the Isle of Benfar, get his own tenants, and create a small, self-sustaining community. There was enough land to farm, so they wouldn't depend on food and supplies from the mainland. They could raise sheep and sell wool and hides to earn coin, grow flax and make and sell linen. While he'd have tenants and farmers on the island, he'd make sure they wouldn't disturb him unless necessary, and he'd farm his own land and live peacefully alone.

When Hamish announced he'd come to see the warden about a job, the guard let him through the gates and behind the walls. Household buildings stood around the courtyard: stables, a chicken pen, an ale brewery, a bakery. The two-story, gray-stone house had a big, round tower on one corner. To let a little light in, windows had sheets made of stretched animal horn that had been soaked for months. The building reminded Hamish of a small castle.

The guard led Hamish to the dark stables, and warm air

enveloped him as he walked inside. The scent of horses and hay was comforting. Back on the farm, working with animals had been his escape from his cruel parents, and Hamish had loved taking care of horses, cows, and sheep. A goose honked angrily, and Hamish saw the white bird in the corner. Odd. Why would a goose be here and not in the pen?

Someone was shouting, and Hamish saw a large man leaning over someone smaller.

"You shod the horse wrong," the man boomed. "You almost maimed it. If that happens again, I will kick you out, and you will never find work in Cumbria."

Did he just threaten a wee lad? Anger rose in Hamish like a hot wall of fire. He wouldn't allow anyone to mistreat children. Not after what his adoptive parents had done to Fiona. Hamish clenched his fists. The man shoved the small person, who then stumbled and ran past Hamish.

Not a lad. A short, skinny man. Hamish stared at the large figure. The man approached him and came into the light. He was tall, almost as tall as Hamish—and Hamish had never met a man as tall as him. The man had a meaty nose and puffy lips, and a stomach as big as an ale barrel. His eyes sat deep in his sockets under the heavy lids of someone who didn't mind a few cups of ale or wine every night. He had thick dark-blond hair streaked with silver and the well-groomed beard of a man of high status.

"Warden," Hamish said.

Warden George Tailor slowly looked him over with an estimating expression of cloudy gray eyes.

"Who are you?" he said with an English accent.

"My name is Hamish. I heard ye're looking for a man for a job."

"Black Hamish himself?" He rubbed his chin. "I've heard of you."

Hamish cocked his head. "Before ye tell me anything, ye should ken there's two things I dinna do. I dinna harm women and I dinna harm children. Does yer assignment involve any of that?"

"No."

Hamish lifted one shoulder. "Then I'm certain we can come to an agreement."

Tailor folded his arms over his broad chest. "How well do you know the situation in the Borderlands?"

On the Marches, the border between England and Scotland, battles and clashes between the English and the Scots were constant. It was up to the Scottish earls and the English lord wardens of the Marches to keep peace and order. The Borderlands were divided into West, Middle, and East Marches. Pretty much destroyed by the Wars of Scottish Independence, the whole region struggled, living in poverty.

It would be best to conceal how much Hamish knew, that way, mayhap something useful would slip from Tailor's mouth.

"Canna say I ken it well," he said.

"Let me explain. I was appointed by the king to come here from the south of England to be a warden of the English Western March. The chief of the Maxwell clan, from Castle Caerlaverock, is the warden of the Scottish West March."

Deidre's father had been appointed as a warden? What did that mean to Deidre? He'd hoped it meant she had more security and a better position. If she was marrit and lived with her husband, it wouldn't matter that much.

Tailor walked towards a beautiful brown horse and patted its nose. Its nostrils flared while it sniffled him. "Surely you've heard the reputation of these lands? Scots raid us. We raid Scots. Thieves and highwaymen raid everyone regardless. I've been appointed by the king to bring order and peace to these lands." He looked sharply at Hamish. "But how am I to do that if the warden of Scottish West March and his clan are raiders themselves?"

Deidre's father? A reiver? Surely that was just a rumor? He was the chief of a powerful clan. "How can ye be certain?"

"My trusted man recognized the chief when he raided a village nearby. Despite the agreement between the wardens to fight this sort of nonsense, Maxwell is actually the one instigating it." He scoffed and hit a board of the stables wall with his fist. "Well, he isn't going to do that for long. This is where I need you."

Something cold coiled in Hamish's gut. "I'm listening."

Tailor met Hamish's eyes, and in them, there wasn't anger or rage. There was a stone-cold emptiness. Hamish didn't care much about anyone or anything except himself, but this emptiness chilled him to the bone.

"I need you to kill Harris Maxwell," Tailor said in an even voice, as though he talked about how much snow had fallen today. "And I need you to make it appear as though clan Johnstone did it. If the reivers are fighting one another, they won't have time to raid my lands. They won't steal anything from me, and the king will be happy with my services. My family will live peacefully. My wife has just had a third baby, for God's sake."

Killing Harris Maxwell—Deidre's father... Could he do that to her? Even if she weren't his, he still loved her.

No. He didn't. He'd thought he loved her, but he was wrong. He didn't love. Loving meant giving in to emotions and losing control. Losing control meant pain. It meant he'd lose people who were dear to him. He wouldn't go through that again. After Fiona died, and he'd killed her murderers with his bare hands, he'd swore to himself that he'd never go through a loss like that again.

Besides, Deidre was no one to him anymore. She must be another man's wife by now. And yet it still felt wrong to take the job. "I will. For the right price."

"And what is the right price?"

"Ten pounds." The sum was exorbitant. A knight's yearly wages were about fifteen pounds. It was twice what Hamish had asked from John MacDougall for the job in Inverlochy Castle. There, he'd needed to infiltrate Robert the Bruce's army and discover the secret tunnel. It would be enough to secure the land on the Isle of Benfar.

After his years living and working as his adoptive parents' slave on the farm, and after they'd all but killed Fiona, he knew he would never let anyone use him like that again. The way to ensure that never happened was a complete independence, complete control over his environment. What better place to do that than on his own island?

Tailor's eyes widened and then narrowed, and Hamish had the strangest sensation of his neck being in a vise.

"No," Tailor said.

But Hamish knew it wasn't a no. Tailor was just negotiating.

"Fine." Hamish turned around. "Goodbye."

He'd reached the door of the stables when Tailor said, "Wait."

Hamish looked over his shoulder.

"I'll give you the ten pounds. But only after it's all done, and I hear the news from someone else."

Hamish turned around. "Fair enough."

"The bishop of Carlisle made the wardens agree to hold the truce for the twelve days of Christmas to let the locals have a rest and some hope. If peace is broken, the bishop will be very angry, and if the bishop is angry, there'll be trouble with the king. I'm new here, but I firmly intend to stay for a long time. I need you to kill him on Christmas Day, when no one will suspect any malice. The bishop of Carlisle will come to dine with my family, so he will never suspect me."

Hamish cocked his head. "Aye. Can be done."

Tailor straightened his belt on his large stomach. "Good. I expect a report from you daily. Wait here for a while before you leave so no one knows we were here together, understood?"

"Aye. Understood." Hamish smirked to himself. Careful, calculating bastart.

Tailor nodded, and without throwing another glance at Hamish, he walked out. The goose on a pile of hay in the corner honked. Growing up on the farm on the Isle of Skye, he'd always loved interacting with the animals. He hadn't minded cleaning the pens and stables as a boy because he'd enjoyed talking with the animals.

"Are ye sitting on eggs?" he said. "Isna it early?"

The goose replied with a displeased honking tirade.

Hamish shook his head with a chuckle. "All right, but dinna get too attached to them. If they hatch, the winter mayhap get them. Ah well, mayhap ye'll become Christmas dinner yerself before yer heart is broken."

The goose honked in protest but kept sitting.

"Suit yerself. I warned ye."

After a short while, he decided enough time had passed and he made his way outside. He opened the door, and the last light of dusk filtered into the stables. He glanced at the goose, then without looking, he stepped outside and stumbled right into someone.

They almost fell, but he caught delicate shoulders in his embrace and steadied the woman. When he saw her face, his heart stopped.

A brown stardust of freckles covered the woman's nose and cheeks. Her bronze hair was hidden under a hood. Her icy-blue eyes stared at him, and he was sure the same astonishment was written all over his own face.

Deidre.

CHAPTER 2

Deidre's whole body stilled, as though it had ceased to exist.

No. Wrong. On the contrary. It was as though she'd been reborn. The courtyard was quiet, the stables grew darker, but the snow on the ground and on the roofs of the buildings was so white it hurt her eyes. The scent of woodsmoke from the kitchen disappeared, replaced by the scent of Hamish's manly musk, snow, and horses. The honking of a goose, the soft snorting of horses, and the voices from the market square behind the wall all grew quieter.

He was big. Tall, all-consuming, and larger than life.

Dark and dangerous and heart-wrenching.

"Hamish," she whispered.

He stood in the doorway of the dark stables, devouring her with his eyes, the dark pools as black as the loch at night. Every hair on her body stood, as though charged with the energy of a lightning bolt. The hands that held her shoulders in place radiated heat even through the layers of clothing.

"Deidre..." he purred.

Oh Jesu, Mary, and Joseph! The man she'd never thought she'd see again stood before her.

The man who'd broken her heart and her life.

He was the reason she was here working for the warden's wife.

The reason her daughter had grown up fatherless.

She stepped back, escaping his grasp. He blinked and stared at his empty hands for a moment.

A burning fear for her daughter sizzled in the pit of her stomach. This was bad. She wouldn't let him hurt Maeve like he'd hurt her.

Deidre glanced back at the courtyard, making sure Maeve was nowhere to be seen. All she saw was the kitchen boy taking scraps to the pigs. "What are ye doing here?"

"I-" he said and closed his mouth.

She could take pride in making Hamish speechless.

"Why are *ye* here?" he asked. "Ye aren't the warden's wife, are ye?" A threat in his voice rumbled like a distant thunder.

"'Tis nae yer concern whose wife I am. But nae. I'm nae marrit to him."

He looked her up and down, the puzzled frown on his face making his thick eyebrows knit together and his eyes darken under them. No doubt he wondered why she wore the clothes of a poor woman. Why her cloak wasn't trimmed with fur, but had holes and patches on it. Why she wore her shoes until the wrinkles in the leather turned to holes. Clearly, she did not look the way a chief's daughter should.

He, however, looked better than she remembered. Aye, he'd aged, and judging by the sword behind his back with its antler hilt, the good quality of his woolen cloak, and his new boots, he wasn't a poor, young man anymore, but a man with purpose and experience. He'd gained more scars on his face. A silver one crossed his left eyebrow like a claw. His nose was slightly crooked. Another thin silver scar ran across his right cheekbone like the narrow trickle of a brook.

And those eyes... She could tell that he'd seen more darkness than she could ever imagine.

"Are ye a servant?" he asked.

"A wet nurse."

He blinked. "A wet nurse? Ye?"

"For the lady's youngest, aye."

"Do ye have a bairn, too, then?"

She stepped back, panic gripping her throat. She didn't want him to know of Maeve's existence. But she probably shouldn't worry at all. Most likely, he wouldn't even care. Wouldn't throw a second glance at the girl.

Still. What if he suddenly wanted to be in their lives?

"Ye lost the right to ken and ask anything when I pretty much begged ye to marry me and ye abandoned me all those years ago."

He pressed his lips tightly together in his beard. "Ye will answer me."

"I wilna. What are ye doing here, anyway?" she pressed.

Please, say ye're already leaving.

He glared at her. "The warden has hired me for a mission." Something dark flickered across his face, something resembling guilt.

"Will ye be here for a long time?"

"Nae. Only until the Night of Candles."

"Well, good. The less I see ye the better. I wish I didna see ye at all."

She spun on her heel and marched towards the big house, but Hamish caught her by the elbow and turned her to face him.

"Deidre, what happened to ye? Why are ye a wet nurse?"

Bitterness rose in her throat. "Between that or selling my body for the pleasures of men, I'd rather feed a bairn with my milk."

"But why are ye nae with yer family? Or marrit to an important man?"

She freed her elbow from his grasp and shook her head, hot tears springing from her eyes. "Why do ye think? My family doesna want to have anything to do with me. My father, who I thought loved me more than anything, chased me away."

She tightened her fists to stop the violent shaking of her hands. "All because of ye," she spat the words like they were poisoned.

The look of surprise mixed with guilt on his face was a rare sight. He opened his mouth to say something, but if she heard another word from him, she might burst with venom.

Or worse.

She might tell him exactly why her station in life had changed so dramatically. And she wouldn't put her daughter in danger by knowing a cruel man like Hamish.

She picked up the skirts of her dress and ran inside the house as far away from Hamish as possible.

CHAPTER 3

December 21, 1308

Hamish arrived at Caerlaverock early the next day.

The previous glory of the proud castle was gone. Instead, he stared at a half-ruined construction in the middle of a frozen moat. When Hamish had visited it with Sir Cope nine years ago, the castle had represented all the latest advancements and was the pride of the Maxwell clan. It had made them one of the most powerful clans in the Lowlands. A force to reckon with.

Now half of the castle stood in ruins.

What had happened? Hamish remembered the impressive gatehouse with its two thick, round towers with slit windows flanking the entrance and the drawbridge over the moat. Not many castles in Scotland had gatehouses. It was most definitely an innovation of Norman influence. From behind the towers, the walls had been built to angle off to the left and right. From a bird's eye, the castle would probably look like a triangle.

The gatehouse had clearly come under fire. The wooden gallery on top of the ramparts was gone, and soot blackened the tops of the towers. The left tower looked as though a giant knife had cut it diagonally, and remnants of the chief's chamber were visible on the second floor. The wall on the right side had a gap in it. The moat was filled with rocks, bundles of sticks, and dirt to create a makeshift bridge where the drawbridge used to lie at the castle gate.

A bad feeling weighed heavily in Hamish's gut. Was this because of the wars with the Bruce?

Did Deidre know about this?

Deidre... On the ride here, she'd occupied his mind. She aged, aye, but nae like a flower would dry and die out. Before, she'd been skinny, in a youthful way. Now, her figure had rounded out and she glowed. Her inner fire had hardened into steel.

She took his breath away.

He had so many questions, and the damned lass wouldn't give him any answers. How was he responsible for her being rejected by her family? Why did she work as a wet nurse? When he'd left, only Innis and Simon had known about their affair. Had Deidre confessed to her mother or father?

That wasn't his fault. He'd thought he was doing her a favor by leaving her to marry a rich, important man so that she'd be protected and taken care of. A life on the road with him without a home wasn't the life for a highborn lady.

He must have been twelve years old when he left the farm. He went down south, begging, stealing food and coin, running away from the soul-crushing pain of having lost Fiona, and not knowing what he wanted to do. He'd reached England, where people were wealthier, and he'd learned the language and the accent, learned to blend in and be invisible.

One day, a knight saw him fighting. Instead of punishing Hamish, he'd been impressed with Hamish's strength and cleverness and offered him a position as his squire. He'd paid nothing, but he'd given Hamish food, clothes, a roof over his head, and he'd taught Hamish to fight.

Years later, after the knight died in a tournament, Hamish decided he didn't want to be a knight and hired himself out as a mercenary. Someone had needed a man to convince his neighbor to stop disputing some land. Hamish had done it efficiently, and he'd liked scaring people instead of it being the other way around. Little by little, he'd gotten similar "dirty" jobs that no one else wanted—scaring, threatening, blackmailing, stealing. His name was soon spoken in whispers, and he'd begun to get bigger jobs. Assassination paid the best, and he started to realize his dream of living on his own island might actually come true.

He clicked his tongue and let the horse carefully walk towards the castle and over the filling in the moat. The horse's hooves sank into the muddy mix of dirt and snow.

"Who goes there?" came a call from above.

Oh good. At least they still had guards on the gate.

"'Tis Hamish Dunn," he called. "Chief Maxwell kens me."

No answer came back, and Hamish assumed it would take a while for the man to fetch the chief.

"Hamish Dunn?" replied the voice.

"Aye." Hamish stared up the tower, trying to distinguish the speaker.

"Wait."

He dismounted and waited for a while, then the gate opened. Harris Maxwell stood there with a sword on his belt. He'd aged. His hair was a dull bronze mixed with silver and was long enough to hang to his shoulder blades. His gray beard was full. Deidre had his eyes—icy blue and piercing, smart and entirely unforgettable.

They were the eyes of a predator on a hunt, and they stayed with ye.

"'Tis been a long time," Harris said, and Hamish realized it was the same voice he'd heard from the tower.

"Aye." Hamish looked him over, assessing how strong of a warrior he still was.

"Come. Have ye traveled from afar?"

He stepped aside and let Hamish lead his horse inside. The courtyard spoke of how bad things were for the Maxwells. The chicken pen was charred, one wall of the stables was missing, and wooden planks were hammered to it in a patchwork repair. A big crack ran through the wall on the opposite side. The tower had a hole in the wall, too.

Nine years ago, he'd ridden into the glorious courtyard through the gates after Sir Cope. Harris, his wife and three daughters stood in line to greet the guests. Last one was Deidre. Thin and bronze-haired, her eyes the color of the winter sky, huge and shiny. Everything around him had frozen, as though turning to ice.

He hadn't been able to look away. He'd never seen a woman as beautiful as her. She'd ignited in him the fire of a blacksmith's furnace that had the ability to melt iron.

"What happened here?" Hamish asked as a servant came to take his horse.

Harris walked into the undamaged gatehouse tower and Hamish followed him.

"The English, that's what happened," Harris threw across his shoulder. "We supported the Bruce in the beginning, so they took our castle. Now, as long as we support the English occupying Galloway and the south of Scotland, we can stay."

They came into what was probably serving as the great hall, although there were only a few tables for guests. The lord's table was there, however, together with the great chair.

Harris's wife, Lady Laire, sat at the lord's table with her embroidery. Three English warriors were at the other table, their backs bent as they wolfed down something that looked like sludge. They clunked the cutlery against the bowls as they ate. The scent of cooked cabbage and onions hung in the air.

The real great hall, with its embroidered clan sigil and

arms, intricate carvings on the chief's great chair, and many tables for the clan and guests must have been destroyed in the other tower.

"They laid sieged and took my castle, as ye see. They almost destroyed it. They garrison here whenever they wish." He pointed with his chin towards the three warriors. "My men were either killed or left. Only a handful are still here."

That was good for Hamish's mission. The less men to guard their chief, the better. Though the English garrison could be a problem. But he would work around them.

They sat down at another table, separate from Lady Maxwell and the English warriors. Lady Maxwell threw a glance at Hamish that was both fearful and antagonistic. She must not enjoy the talks of politics and war.

The surface of the table felt sticky under Hamish's fingers and smelled of old ale. The air was cold and drafty despite the lit fireplace. Biting his upper lip, he looked around the vaulted ceiling and the stone walls with its broken wooden paneling. Two red zigzagging patterns circled the walls above the level of the slit windows. An old, dusty tapestry depicting a hunt scene hung from the wall opposite the fireplace. That must be the work of Deidre's mother or sisters. Deidre hated embroidering.

"Where are yer daughters?" Hamish said.

Harris's shoulders tensed ever so slightly. "They're well. Marrit. Thank God they dinna have to see this."

Marrit? Was Deidre marrit, too? So why was she serving as a wet nurse, then? Surely if she'd marrit anyone, it would be a rich man, and she wouldn't need to work.

"What about Deidre?"

Harris scratched his forehead, lowered his head, and looked down. Those were signs he was ashamed.

"Deidre, too, aye." Harris jerked his shoulder and shifted on his seat. He was lying.

So she wasn't marrit. What the hell had happened between her family and her, then?

If the man had chased Deidre away for whatever reason, shameful or nae, and left her alone for the life of a poor woman who might need to prostitute herself, Hamish wouldn't hesitate to kill him.

"Good." Hamish cleared his throat to swallow down his anger. This was not the time nor the place to raise any suspicions. "Things are nae good for ye, I see."

"Nae, man. But I still have my core band of men to keep things in order."

"Order? Borderlands still swarm with thieves and thugs. I was almost robbed on my way down from the north."

"If 'twas any of my men, I'm sorry."

"Yer men?"

Harris sighed, glanced around, then leaned forward. "Aye. Between us, I have to raid, Hamish. I hate that, but ye see what happened to my castle and my lands. 'Tis the only way to sustain my clan."

Hamish blinked. So he wasn't raiding because of greed. He raided because he needed to eat and feed his wife and his men.

"But ye still swore an allegiance to the English king?" Hamish said.

"Aye. But I hear the Bruce is doing well up north? If he can help me get my freedom back from these bloodsuckers, I will swear to him on my life."

Hamish nodded. After the Battle of the Pass of Brander, where Hamish had fought against the Bruce because he'd been hired by the English side, he'd started doubting his neutrality. He'd seen the power of loyalty and faith, the power of fighting for something greater than himself.

His whole life, he'd only fought for the money in his pocket because money meant freedom. Money meant control. Honor and other idealistic shite didn't matter to him. He was a selfish bastart, aye. And he was pretty happy with that. He'd done many things in his life he'd burn in hell for. Hurting women and children was the only line he hadn't crossed.

Hamish needed to find out what he would be dealing with on Christmas Day. "Is Lady Laire planning anything for the celebrations?"

"Aye. She's invited the Johnstone, Urwin, and Grame clans."

Good. There would be enough people for him to easily lay blame on the clan Johnstone.

"May I come, as well?" he said. "Forgive me for inviting myself, but I dinna have anywhere to go."

"Oh, aye. I'm sure Laire wilna mind."

"Thank ye."

"Aye. Now let me pour ye some ale." He walked to another table and brought back a clay jar and two cups. "Tell me, Hamish, how is old Sir Cope? What have ye been doing all this time?"

Although this mission appeared easy, Hamish didn't yet know if he could actually bring himself to kill Deidre's father. He watched the old man pour the ale and wondered if knowing what had happened between Harris and Deidre would make things easier or more difficult for him.

CHAPTER 4

December 22, 1308

DEIDRE PUT THE WARM, SLEEPY STEPHEN INTO HIS COT, inhaling the sweet scent of the baby, a mixture of milk and a soft, flowery aroma that was unique to each bairn. Maeve had smelled like apple blossoms as a newborn, something Deidre would never have thought while she was pregnant with her. When the midwife had put baby Maeve on Deidre's chest, she'd never been more torn between absolute love for the bairn and hurt from being abandoned. She'd missed Hamish every day of her pregnancy, but never as much as she'd missed him when their daughter was born.

But enough! Seeing him yesterday had been quite the shock. She wouldn't think of him again. She had work to do and a daughter to think of.

The nursery was a large room, in semidarkness now. Only rich people like the Tailors could afford a separate room for children. Alice, who was ten, and Lucia, who was five, slept in the room with little Stephen, too, but they were with their mother now. The girls slept in a bed with an elaborate canopy and beautiful red curtains. Deidre and Maeve slept on a small bed in the corner, since Deidre had to nurse Stephen at night. Chests with toys stood along the walls. There was also a table with a small wooden bath where Stephen was bathed several times a day after he soiled himself. Maeve hadn't had that luxury at his age and had often had a skin rash. The room smelled fresh because the chambermaid cleaned it daily.

The bairn wore a satisfied expression, and Deidre carefully wiped a drop of milk that rolled out of the corner of his mouth with a linen cloth. He'd always been an eager eater and sported adorable fat rolls on his chubby arms and legs. Deidre's breasts had never been fuller with any of the five bairns she'd previously nursed.

Stephen was six months old and just started to eat porridge and strained vegetables, but his appetite for milk hadn't diminished, surprisingly. He was a fussy bairn and liked the comfort of nursing, and she wondered if he thought of her as his mother. Even if the bairns she'd nursed weren't hers, she loved them. She was satisfied knowing she'd provided them with warmth and nutrition and kept them well and alive. Sometimes as she nursed, she'd catch Stephen's mother gazing at her with an intense burning expression. Was Matilda jealous of her? Deidre knew she'd hate to see another woman feed her child.

Deidre and Maeve had lived through a year of poverty with Innis's small family. Innis and Simon had barely had enough food on their table, and they'd often been cold and hungry. Through it all, Deidre had reveled in the love of her daughter.

Rejected by her own clan, Deidre had cuddled the sweet, warm body of her daughter and felt that she and Maeve were alone against the world. The baby had cooed and gazed at her as though she were a miracle, a star, the moon and the sun.

Even in the darkest moments of despair, Deidre had just needed to look into her daughter's eyes to know that she'd be strong for her and make it no matter what. She'd crawled out of that situation and provided for her child, protected her, and she would never let anyone hurt Maeve like Hamish had hurt her.

Where was Maeve now?

It was time for the midday meal, and the whole household was probably busting about the lord and lady's meal in the great hall. Deidre threw a last glance at Stephen who sighed ever so slightly, his puffy lips parted.

Deidre was fortunate that her employers had agreed to take on both her and her daughter. Most only took in the wet nurse, who then had to leave her own child at home and have a husband or a mother to watch over them. But Deidre had no home and no one to watch Maeve. She made it one of the conditions of her employment. She could only work if her daughter could live with her.

If anyone found out that Maeve was really a bastart, and Deidre was not a widow, but rather the daughter of the Maxwell chief, they'd send her away immediately, and she'd never be able to find work in the Borderlands again.

Luckily, Maeve knew how to keep their secret. She was a sweet girl, a kind and undemanding soul who helped in the household, cleaning after the lord and lady's children, washing their clothes, bringing fresh water for Stephen's baths, straining purees for him.

Every time Deidre looked at her, she saw Hamish. The almost black hair, the dark eyes, and defined, arched eyebrows...

Deidre had a bit of time before Stephen would wake, and she went to look for Maeve. But when she opened the door and stepped out of the nursery, she knocked into a giant wall of a man reeking of roast drippings and ale. She stepped back, mortified.

George Tailor turned around and glared at her with his small, pig eyes.

"Forgive me, my lord." She lowered her head, praying he'd just let her go and attend to whatever business he had.

The man was dangerous. He was convinced he needed to run his household with an iron fist, especially the women, and she'd seen the lady of the house covered in bruises. Every servant in the household knew to keep the lord as happy as possible. There were more beggars on the streets than work available, and the lord wouldn't hesitate to throw a servant out.

"Deidre," he said, and she felt his heavy, probing gaze on her. "How's my son?"

"Asleep, lord. He's a good lad."

She stared right at the floor between her feet and his, and she tensed all over when he stepped towards her. The reek of pig roast and alcohol intensified as his huge frame shielded the light of the oil lamp. His fat finger landed below her chin, and he lifted her face up. Deidre's jaw locked, and her neck muscles strained and stiffened as she fought the urge to knock his hand from her face.

His dark eyes ogled her. His whole face was bloated from daily ale and wine. He slowly looked down her body, his puffy eyes lingering at her breasts.

He smacked his lips as he opened his mouth to speak. "Do you find you're treated well here, Deidre?"

"Aye, my lord."

She was. Her daughter was, too. So far.

"Hmm..." His gaze crawled up and down her face, studying her like a rare piece of silk he was considering buying. "I'm glad to hear that."

He dropped his hand, and she sighed with relief. But he didn't step away from her.

"When did your husband die?" he said.

"Uhm. Right after my daughter was born, my lord."

"How old is she?"

"Eight, my lord."

He cupped her jaw, and Deidre suppressed a gag.

"For eight years, no man has touched a beautiful woman like you..." He brushed her cheek with his thumb. "You must miss it. Your body has needs..."

Deidre locked her knees to stop herself from kicking him between his legs.

"I dinna, my lord. I'm verra content in yer house."

"I don't think you know what you're missing. My wife is a cold English woman. I see a fire in you... These Scottish freckles, this beautiful face..." He stepped even closer to her, his large stomach pressing against hers. He laid his hand on her lower back and drew her to him. "Be my lover, Deidre. I will make it worth your while."

Had she heard him right? Had he just asked her to be his mistress?

To her horror, he lowered his head to kiss her. Deidre tensed, watching his face move to hers slowly, like in a nightmare.

A door opened with a *bang*. They both looked down the hall for the source of the sound. There, illuminated by an oil lamp, stood Hamish.

HAMISH COULDN'T REMEMBER THE LAST TIME HE'D WANTED to kill a man.

He killed on his missions because he had to. Because he was paid for that. He didn't hold personal grudges against his victims. The last time he'd *wanted* to kill someone was back on the Blàrach farm on the Isle of Skye, twenty years ago as he'd held Fiona's cold body in his arms. Bruises had decorated her pale, translucent skin, her golden hair had looked mousy. He'd closed her blue eyes and held her, rocked her, delirious from grief.

Had Bearnas, their adoptive mother, not beaten her so badly, she might not have developed a fever. The only good thing in his life had died. And it had been his adoptive parents' doing.

The black, windowless house had always been full of smoke and the smell of the animals who lived with them for warmth. He'd put Fiona back to bed, ran out of the house, grabbed the ax from the stump for woodcutting and gone looking for the people he believed had ultimately killed Fiona.

He didn't remember much about that day, except that he'd let out the pain, the loss, and the daily humiliation from his childhood. They'd deserved to die for mistreating and abusing Fiona. For breaking his soul.

Seeing George Tailor looming over Deidre like a fat pig over a cat, he felt a wave of burning rage rise within him.

Tailor let her go and stepped away from her. The mixture of panic and anger on her flushed face spurred the rage within Hamish to a new level. He clenched his jaw so tightly his teeth almost cracked. His hands curled into fists.

The horny boar wanted Deidre to become his *mistress*? Hamish suppressed a low growl at the back of his throat.

Tailor's expression changed from annoyance to anger. Without another word to Deidre, he marched towards Hamish, holding him tightly in his glare.

He stopped by the door and threw it open. "How dare you come here uninvited?" he said to Hamish quietly. "Do not talk to me in front of people." With that, Tailor disappeared behind the door.

Deidre stared at Hamish, their eyes locked across the long, dark hall. She lifted her chin high and marched forward. God, she was beautiful. Her eyes flashed almost indigo now in the semidarkness. Her cheeks were flushed, and her hair fell in long, auburn locks.

She almost passed him, but he caught her by the elbow and stopped her. Her scent enveloped him—something sweet and calming and herbal. She smelled of home and babies and love.

His chest ached. Those were all things he craved and were in his reach, but he'd never have them.

"Are ye going to?" he said.

"What?"

"Become his mistress?"

She yanked her arm out of his grasp. "'Tis none of yer concern, Hamish. Ye dinna dare say one word about this. Ye lost yer right long ago. Ye're no one to me."

She pushed through the door and stormed out. No, he wouldn't let her leave just like that. He had to find out what had happened to her. Why her father had lied to him, and why she'd ended up a wet nurse in a horrible man's house.

"Nae, ye dinna walk away from me like that," he growled and followed her. They marched through a dark landing illuminated only by oil lamps and into a large, square courtyard. The household buildings—the animal pen, the kitchen, and the stables—looked black compared to the white snow. The daylight hurt his eyes after the semidarkness of the house. "Ye will answer me."

"Go to hell, Hamish. Go back to wherever ye came from. Ye have a bad habit of ruining my life."

"Ruining yer life? What are ye talking about?"

They marched through the courtyard, and she stopped next to a building that must be the kitchen, judging by the mouthwatering aroma of roasted meat and baked bread. She turned to face him, her mouth pressed in a thin, angry line, her lips white. "Ye left me like a coward all those years ago."

His gut churned, both with frustration and with guilt. "Lass, what would ye have had me do?"

She opened her mouth to say something when a wee lass with a burlap pouch in her hands came out of the kitchen building. She was tall and reminded him of Deidre with her freckles, slim nose, and full lips. She wore a simple brown dress of a servant girl. Her hair was covered with a dirty, grayish cap, and a long, almost black braid showed under it and lay on her shoulder.

"Ma," she said, looking at Deidre and beaming. "I was going to fetch ye some bread after I fed the geese."

Ma...

She was Deidre's daughter.

Deidre glanced at her with wide eyes, horrified.

"Ye *do* have a child," Hamish said.

"Good morrow, lord," the lass said, looking at Hamish.

"Go feed the geese, sweet," Deidre said and pushed the lass slightly towards the pen.

"Good morrow," Hamish replied, stunned.

The lass studied him with a frown and walked on towards the pen. She had Deidre's graceful movements. But who was her father?

"Tell me. Whose is she?" Hamish said.

Christ, what if she was his? Shock froze him. If he knew he had a child, he'd never leave it. Aye, he was a cold bastart, but not to his kin.

Kin.

Having a bairn would mean attaching himself to someone, loving them. Horror trickled down his spine. Loving someone meant pain. Meant loss. He didn't think he'd survive another.

Lifetimes passed between his question and her answer.

"Nae yers," Deidre said.

He didn't think there existed two words that could bring him more relief and pain at the same time.

"Whose then? Were ye marrit?"

She closed her eyes briefly, as though gathering her strength. "If I answer all yer questions, will ye leave us alone once and for all?"

Hamish didn't think that was possible. "Aye."

She sighed. "Aye, I was marrit. He died. Maeve is his."

Hamish gave a curt nod, jealousy scraping at his heart. "Who was he?"

She raised her chin. "A good, simple man."

"Did ye love him?"

Her nostrils flared. "Love doesna matter."

"Deidre. Answer me. Did ye?"

"Again, whether I loved someone or nae isna yer concern."

Wasn't his concern? His cold, calculating mind couldn't agree more. But his body...

His heart pounded like a fist against his rib cage. The thought of her loving someone else pained him physically, making him want to tear that man apart.

Deidre belonged to him. She was his. She was correct that he didn't have any right to demand something of her. He'd let her go and abandoned her. But all that didn't change the fact that he had this howling, aching void that throbbed for her, that shouted she was his. She couldn't love anyone but him. Couldn't marry anyone but him. Couldn't bear anyone's children but his.

"Oh, but 'tis, lass," he growled.

Her eyes flashed with fire, mirroring the same passion that raged in his blood. Oh, she wanted him. She still wanted him. He took her by the shoulders, wrapped his arms around her, and kissed her.

CHAPTER 5

He kissed her...

His mouthed claimed hers like it belonged to him, like it was the most natural thing in the world for them to collide and melt together.

It was just like she remembered. His lips were soft but demanding. His tongue was succulent and wanton. It invaded her, every lick and caress a proclamation that she was his. A hot wave ran through her, impairing her thoughts. Her skin was flushed and burning. His arms were like iron bars around her waist.

Oh sweet Jesu, how she'd missed the allure of his mouth, the safe confinement of his strong arms. It was as though no time had passed, as though he'd never disappeared and never betrayed her. As though this were the first time he'd put his lips on hers.

Like that first time, nine years ago in Caerlaverock, he was so masculine he made her head spin. Like her father's best *uisge*, he was dark and strong and delicious, promising pleasure, adventure, and freedom. But it was also dangerous, betraying her by making her lose her mind.

Look where it had gotten her before.

She'd be a fool to trust him or anyone else but herself and her daughter.

She did what she should have done all those years ago. She pushed him away and slapped him. Her palm stung, and his head jerked to the side. He gasped and slowly turned to her, his nostrils flaring. He pressed his fingers against his cheek. His eyes flashed dangerously, thunderstorms raging behind them. She wasn't afraid of him, even though she knew what he did on his missions.

She would do everything to protect herself and her daughter against this man—or anyone—from the hurt of being abandoned, because that's what Hamish would eventually do when he went off on his next mission.

"Lass..." he said, a threat like thunder in his voice.

"Dinna dare ever do that again. Ye wilna touch me. Ye wilna come close to me or my daughter."

"But I dinna—"

"I dinna want to hear it."

She turned on her heel and went into the pen to gather Maeve and take her back into the nursery. Hamish wouldn't be allowed there, and she would feel safe and be able to take a deep, calming breath. She needed to chase away this molten, unapologetic desire that exposed her and brought her fully and completely at Hamish's mercy.

She just needed to steer clear of him. He'd be gone soon. She had to be strong and resist him. No matter how much her own body wanted to betray her.

HAMISH PETTED HIS HORSE THOUGHTFULLY. AFTER DEIDRE stormed away, he'd talked to Tailor in the stables. He'd told the warden he was invited to Maxwell's castle for Christmas and would be able to finish the job then. He'd only need a sword or a dagger or some object with the Johnstone sigil on it. Tailor promised to deliver.

A heaviness weighed in his heart for having to kill Deidre's father. But a mission was a mission. She'd never know he was the one behind her father's death if he did the part about the Johnstones right. Though whether he could live with himself, he didn't know.

This was exactly why he avoided emotional involvement. Had he not cared about her, he wouldn't hesitate. He wouldn't have this ache in his chest and boulder in his gut. He wouldn't be standing here in the dark stables, inhaling the scent of hay and horse manure, thinking of Deidre and hoping to see her again.

He remembered how after the first kiss, she'd run away from him, breathless and flushed. He'd stood grinning like a young lad. The next day, he'd looked for her, hoping to mayhap see her passing by in the courtyard. During the next few days, they'd only be able to exchange heated, longing glances, but there hadn't been an opportunity to be alone with her.

He'd gone out to see if his snares had caught any hares and heard a rhythmic clash of swords in a grove. He'd hidden behind a tree, careful to remain unseen in case enemies were coming.

Lost in his memory, he remembered his astonishment at seeing it wasn't an enemy attack. It was Deidre and her father, Harris. She was dressed as a man in a tunic and breeches, her long, copper hair in a braid. Her father was attacking her, and she was deflecting his sword. Hamish tensed, ready to protect her if necessary. But it wasn't.

"Stronger, Deidre!" her father cried. "Resist with all the might in yer arms."

She grunted, thrusting her sword to shield her from his attack. Hamish was mesmerized. The lass was breathtaking. She fought like fire, red-cheeked, her blue eyes blazing.

Hamish had never seen a lass fight with a sword. She was so different, and he longed to know her.

The next day, her father asked Hamish to chaperon her to the village nearby. The men of her clan had all gone hunting. Sir Cope had approved, and Hamish had agreed, his heart beating in his throat.

They rode their horses in silence at first, Hamish just marveling at her beauty. Questions swarmed in his head. He was hungry to find out everything about her.

"Why do ye learn to fight?" Hamish said.

She looked at him in surprise, color flushing her cheeks. "How do ye ken?"

"I saw ye and yer da."

"Oh."

"Why dinna ye sit with yer mother and yer sisters in the lady's hall? Dinna women do embroidery or weave linen...or something more fitting for a woman?"

She lifted her chin, thunder behind her eyes. "And why does every woman need to do the same thing? My mother and my sisters can embroider tapestries for every great hall in Scotland."

He could kiss her right now. "So ye dinna want to be like others?"

"Nae." She chuckled. "I dinna. My father teaches me sword-fighting in secret. My mother already says I'm the black sheep in the family."

A black sheep...like him. A black, lonely sheep with no family.

"I want to be independent," she continued. "We live in the Borderlands. Raids and warfare are normal here. If ever, God forbid, my father and his men are unable to protect us, I can."

"I daresay."

"Besides," she said with a shrug, "who says that a woman should only do this or do that. Why should I marry at all if I can protect myself? If I can count and write, which is also something my father taught me secretly, I dinna need a husband."

Hamish studied her, stunned. "A wee rebel, aren't ye? Why did yer da teach ye all that?"

"My mother never gave him a son. I suppose he always wanted to do all those things a father does when he has one."

"Ye *canna* do everything a man does."

"Nae? What canna I do? Tell me."

"I canna tell ye, but I would give much to show ye."

She flared her nostrils and looked straight at him. There was defiance and a challenge and a vulnerability in her icy-blue eyes. "I can do that, too. 'Tis my body. It belongs to me."

Shaking off the memory, Hamish rubbed his cheek where it still burned from her slap. That fire...she still had it. Mayhap, the slap had been well deserved, but it had certainly been worth it. To taste her lips again, to have her, delicate and soft and delicious in his arms. It felt like heaven.

He should stay away from her, for his own sake as well as hers, but instinct told him she needed protection. Hamish had seen many bad men in his life, and a man like Tailor was dangerous.

And if he was threatening Deidre...

Something cracked softly in the warm semidarkness. He stared at the corner where he'd seen the mother goose sitting. No one was there right now, but an egg lay on the bed of straw. The goose must have been slaughtered for dinner. He walked towards the egg and leaned over it. The side was cracked, and the broken shells sunk into the egg a little. They pieces were moving. The gosling was ready to hatch.

"Wee bastart," Hamish muttered, staring at it in wonder.

A wee beak protruded through a crack, and the bird kept wriggling and moving inside the egg. It kept pecking at the crack, ***knock-knock, knock-knock***, but it couldn't break through it. It needed help to hatch. He'd watched chicken and geese hatching as a lad on the Blàrach farm and remembered a mother goose assisted a gosling by removing pieces of the shell. He supposed he could help since no one else was here.

He picked the side of the crack with his nail and bent it back so that it opened fully. A wee brown head appeared in the opening. It wriggled some more and broke completely free from the shell. It fell into the hay nest, which was covered with white feathers. The gosling was a wee thing, its fluff wet and brown. It was clearly helpless. It was quite warm in the stables, but was it warm enough for a goose hatchling?

Hamish took it in his hands, its warm, wet body trembling slightly. He breathed onto the gosling to warm it, and it stopped shaking and looked at him with black eyes still half covered with membranes.

"Where's yer mother?" Hamish said. "Ye need yer mother, friend."

He looked at the door. What if its mother had become dinner? The gosling's fate was probably the same, eventually. Best not to think about the wee thing and let nature take its course. Nothing to do about it, anyway.

He put the gosling back into the nest. To his surprise, the bird stood on its feet. The fluff had dried a little now and became more yellow. It wobbled on pink feet, falling but standing back up and walking towards Hamish.

"Better go back to yer bed, wee birdie," Hamish said and walked towards his horse.

The gosling chirped and followed Hamish, slowly, awkwardly. Hamish sped up. "Dinna follow me, ye wee, silly thing. Go back."

But the gosling kept moving and chirping. "Peep-peep-peep."

Hamish stopped and turned around. "What am I supposed to do with ye? Ye canna follow me everywhere..."

"Peep-peep-peep."

Hamish growled in frustration, picked up the goose, and brought it back to the nest. "Stay here. I must go."

He tsked and waggled his finger at it. He turned around and took a few steps, but the peeping came after him. The bird was again at his feet.

He sank to his knees. "We talked about this. Ye canna come with me. Ye must wait for yer mother."

"Peep-peep-peep." It stared at him with its wee black eyes.

The door opened, letting a whoosh of chilly, winter air inside, and Hamish picked the gosling up to shield it from the cold. Deidre's daughter came in with her wee burlap sack. She stopped as though hitting an invisible wall.

"Lord, ye're still here..." she said and looked at his hands.

Her eyebrows rose to her hairline, and her face lit up in the sweetest smile Hamish had ever seen.

Deidre's smile.

"What's yer name, lass?" Hamish said.

"Maeve, my lord."

She came to Hamish, studying the gosling in his hands and petted the wee gosling's head. "Awww," she cooed. "Did it hatch just now?"

Hamish was in awe looking at this wee lass. Something about her was familiar—and nae just that she resembled Deidre... There was something else. Her black hair. Black eyes. Something squeezed in his gut almost painfully.

Nae. She couldn't be his. There were many men with black hair and black eyes.

"Aye," Hamish said. "It did. The wee thing keeps following me."

The lass looked up at him, and a smile spread on her face. "It thinks ye're his mother."

Hamish couldn't ever remember blushing, but heat crept onto his cheeks and neck now. Like a bloody virgin!

He cleared his throat again and shoved the gosling into Maeve's hands. "Here. Take it. 'Tis yers. Where is its mother, anyway?"

She accepted the bird and brought it close to her face to

study it. The gosling kept peeping. "I dinna ken. I came to feed her. She made her nest here in the late fall and refused to leave this place for the pen where the rest of the geese are."

Suddenly, her face went blank, and she looked at Hamish with wide eyes. "Ye dinna think they butchered her for dinner?"

Hamish sucked in a breath. He wished he could shield this precious, sweet lass from the horrors of life, from the notion of death that had accompanied Hamish wherever he went. But he couldn't. Death was everywhere. And household birds were especially prone to it.

"They might have, lass. I'm sorry. Better to nae get attached to this one, either. They all become dinner sooner or later."

Sadness filled Maeve's eyes, and Hamish hated himself for putting it there.

"Then I'll be its mother," she said firmly. "Unless ye want to be."

Hamish chuckled. "'Tis all yers, lass. Ye'll be a great mother goose."

"I think so."

She put the gosling back on the nest and poured some milled grain on a wee board. The gosling began feeding.

Hamish stared at the back of the lass's head. The familiarity of her gestures and movements clawed at his heart.

"Who is yer father?"

"He died, my lord." She glanced back at him. "My mother said I'm nae supposed to talk to ye."

"About yer father?"

"At all."

Hamish nodded. "I wilna bite. Dinna fash about me. Yer mother and I are old acquaintances, and she holds a grudge against me. But I wilna harm yer or her. I just want to ken who yer da is."

She turned back to the gosling and continued to study it. "I dinna ken who he was. He died before I was born. My mother doesna talk of him, at all, nae matter how many times I've asked."

Mayhap it was true, but something wasn't right about this whole story. Did Deidre marry someone from a poor background, and her family reject her because of that? Then why wasn't Deidre with his family?

"Ye're a good lass," Hamish said.

He sat down by her and looked into her eyes.

"If anyone harms ye or yer mother, ye tell me, aye? I will make sure ye and her are safe."

The words came fast, and he could not stop them. Aye, he didn't want to get attached to Deidre and her daughter. But he also couldn't live with himself if any harm came to them if he could have prevented it.

"Thank ye, my lord," she said and smiled.

His heart melted at that smile, and he knew in that moment that he was ready to turn over the world for this sweet, wee lass. Just like that gosling had imprinted on him, so had he on Maeve. Even if she wasn't his, she was Deidre's. And that was enough to bring him to his knees.

CHAPTER 6

Deidre stared at the wee bird in her daughter's hands.

"Why are ye holding a gosling, sweet?" she said.

Maeve marched into the nursery, her cheeks reddening. She hid her eyes, and Deidre knew that meant she'd done something she shouldn't have.

"Because I'm its mother goose."

The bird chirped. Stephen looked at it with curiosity and cooed, excited. Deidre held him on her lap while he chewed on a wooden ring.

"Its what?" Deidre said.

"Its mother goose. It just hatched and started following that man ye were talking to."

Deidre gasped. "Hamish?"

"Aye. Lord Hamish."

Fear froze her hands and feet. "What were ye doing talking to him when I explicitly told ye—"

"I wasna talking to him, Ma. I went to feed the goose that nested in the stables, and he was there, holding this wee birdie."

Lord, give me strength... Deidre closed her eyes. That

sounded exactly like Hamish. The lonely wolf with a warm heart. He was ruthless and hard with his enemies, but he wouldn't harm an innocent woman or a child. Even if that child was a goose.

It's why she'd fallen in love with him. Aye, it had been lust at first that had drawn her to him, but as she'd gotten to know him during the months he stayed in Carlisle after finishing his service with Sir Cope, she'd found out he was a complex riddle. He accepted her the way she was, with all her strange views, her need for independence, and her strong will. Something a typical man would try to break.

He hadn't argued with her. He'd asked questions and studied her like she were an exotic animal. With Hamish, she didn't feel caged like she did with her mother. She'd felt cherished, appreciated, and loved.

She experienced that for the six months that Hamish had been in her life. On the day he left, it was gone forever. She'd become a caged animal again, trying to fit in with the sheep to survive.

What if he gave her daughter that same feeling? The feeling that everything was possible, only to stomp on her hope and crush her world?

Deidre stood with Stephen, then put him in his cot. He turned on his belly and kept munching the ring, staring at Deidre with his big, beautiful baby eyes. Deidre came to kneel by Maeve's side. "Sweet lass," she said, taking her daughter's shoulders in her arms. "He's dangerous. He will tell ye anything, and might... He might..."

"Might what? He said he'd protect ye and me. He said to come to him if anything threatens us."

Deidre suppressed a groan. Of course he'd say that, and he would protect them. He'd kill for them, that wasn't even a question.

Deidre's worry was that he'd never commit. He may be

here to protect them now, but once he'd done whatever it was he'd been hired to do, he wouldn't give them a second glance. He'd say something like "*I thought we had an understanding...*" and then "*The only way to keep control is to be alone. 'Tis my way.*" That was what he'd told her all those years ago.

He didn't need Deidre. He didn't need Maeve. He didn't need anyone, and he wanted to be alone.

Besides, only a selfish, lonely man could encourage a lass to take care of a pet that would bring mess that might anger the warden and his lady.

"He won't be here forever," she said. "Besides, we dinna need protection. I can protect us. Ye ken that, aye?"

"Aye, Ma."

"Now, please get this bird out of the nursery."

"But—"

"Maeve, my dear lass, it poops. We dinna need poop here where wee Stephen is. Lady Matilda wouldna like it."

Maeve's shoulders hung. "Aye. Forgive me, Ma, I didna think of that."

Deidre kissed her on the cheek. "'Tis all right, ye have too kind a heart. Get the gosling back to the pen."

"Maccus."

"What?"

"Its name is Maccus. 'Twas a Norse chief that lived nearby many years ago. Alice told me the story."

Deidre's skin chilled. It was a Maxwell legend that the clan originated from Maccus Well, a pool in the River Tweed. Maccus was a Norse chief who lived during the reign of King David I of Scotland. Quite a coincidence that Maeve had picked that name without knowing her origin, that she belonged to clan Maxwell.

"Sweet child, ye canna name it."

"I can if I'm its mother goose."

Deidre sighed. She wished she didn't need to be so strict

with Maeve. She wished she could give her everything her heart desired.

"Please take it to the pen."

"Aye."

"Dinna fash, sweet, ye can visit it."

"Aye. It follows me, but 'tis cold outside."

"We need to start Christmas preparations. Lady Matilda asked us to decorate the nursery and the kitchens with holly."

Christmas... Would her family celebrate the Night of Candles? Would there be meat pies, a roasted goose, and burning of the Yule log? Were there still holly bushes growing before the bridge as means of protection against witches and evil faeries?

She'd probably never know. She missed the sense of family, the closeness, and the sense of trust she'd been sure could never be broken.

Now she knew all too well that it could. Hamish had taught her that. She'd be a fool to ignore that lesson.

Later that evening, when all the children were sound asleep, Deidre finally went to have her supper. She ate in the kitchen while the cooks scrubbed it clean after the working day. She sat alone at the massive table in the center of the room. The huge fireplace with glowing ambers radiated the scent of woodsmoke and grilled fat. Right under the upper part of the fireplace, fish hung to dry. An oven made of rough stones had been built in the corner. Pots and pans stood on a table alongside the wall.

Her shoulders ached after a day of taking care of the babe, and her fingers prickled from cutting the holly branches for decorations. She walked outside and huddled into her cloak as the frosty air bit her cheeks. She needed to hurry to the main house to cuddle in the warm bed with her daughter and fall into an exhausted sleep.

The night sky was clear, and the moon shone brightly, turning the snow on the roofs and the ground silvery blue.

Snow crunched under her shoes as she walked along the kitchen wall.

As she reached the corner, a shadow lurked to her right. Someone grabbed her by the elbow and tugged her behind the corner of the building.

CHAPTER 7

Deidre gasped, and a hand lay on her mouth, blocking a scream. A strong arm wrapped around her shoulders like an iron rod. She thrust and beat against her capturer. They were hidden from the courtyard behind the kitchen. The outer wall of the estate was ten or so steps away, mayhap if she managed to scream, a passerby would hear her?

"Shhhh, lass," said Hamish's voice in her ear. "'Tis me. I must talk to ye."

A combination of excitement and anger rolled in her stomach. He wanted to talk to her? How dare he snatch her like this. She growled against his hand, thrusting her elbows back into his torso. But he was too strong.

"Stop this, I just want to talk to ye. I ken ye told me this already, but I must ask again. Is Maeve mine?"

Horror froze her, and she stood completely still and breathless in his arms.

"I will let ye go, aye? Dinna scream."

He released his grasp and turned her around. He loomed over her, black and dangerous against the light of the silver moon, his breath puffing out in quick clouds of steam. Wolfish eyes under thick, arched eyebrows stared at her with the intensity of a blazing sun.

"Is she mine?"

"How do ye..."

"She looks like me."

Oh damnation, damnation, damnation!

"I told ye, I was marrit, and she's my dead husband's."

He cocked his head and narrowed his eyes. "Oh, aye? What's his name?"

Her stomach churned. Hamish was many things. Stupid was not one of them. "Jacob Shephard."

"A Sassenach?" He shook his head once. "And when was the wedding?"

She swallowed and scratched her forehead. "In January."

"And why did ye get marrit?"

"Because I loved him. I told ye I wouldna marry without love."

"Hm. And how did ye meet?"

"He..."

Damn him! She hadn't thought all of this through.

"Ye're lying, lass." Hamish lifted her chin with his fingers and looked at her with tenderness. "I ken ye. Ye canna lie."

Deidre's face and neck flushed with heat despite the frosty air. She opened her mouth, desperately searching for an excuse or a clever lie, something that would help her climb out of this mess she'd buried herself in. But nothing came.

"She's mine, isna she?" There was so much softness in his voice that her chest tensed and ached.

How she'd craved to hear him say he'd marry her in that exact voice, that he'd take her and the bairn, and they'd be a family.

Her shoulders went limp. Suddenly, she was too tired. So tired of lying, of being afraid of being discovered, of the constant threat of shame that hung over her head for having given birth to a bastart, for losing her virginity before a wedlock.

She was tired of being alone, of carrying this burden in a life she wasn't supposed to live, of taking care of a child with no support.

Just hearing someone say a gentle word to her... And not just anyone, but the only man she'd ever loved. The only man she wanted to hear tender words from...

She nodded. "Aye."

The word flew out of her mouth on a white puff of steam that dissolved in the black air between them.

HAMISH SUCKED IN A BREATH, ASTONISHED AT THE POWER OF a single word. One word had just changed his life forever. One word had just sent all his reservations and plans crumbling down.

He had a child. The woman he loved had borne his child. That beautiful, dark-haired, kind lass with stardust on her cheeks was his daughter.

But that meant that he'd left Deidre pregnant and alone nine years ago.

"Is that why yer clan rejected ye?" he said.

She sighed and nodded, looking down at her shoes in the snow. She didn't look like the fiery lass he knew her as. Her shoulders rolled inward, and she became smaller, as though she coiled around herself in an attempt to protect her heart. Was that how she'd looked when they'd chased her away? Small, ashamed, rejected, and hurt.

Without the protection of her father, a single, pregnant woman in the Borderlands—how had she survived? Where had she lived with no money and no support? She could have died of poverty, of hunger, of cold—and it would have been his fault.

Hurt and anger rose in him in a crushing wave. "Why didna ye tell me? I would have protected ye. I would have—"

Her icy-blue eyes flashed indigo in the cold night. "Protected me? Ye didna want to do anything with me. Ye told me I was naive to hope ye'd marry me, that ye'd never promised me anything."

Hamish clenched his jaw so tightly his teeth almost cracked. "Ye robbed me of years with my daughter. Ye didna give me a chance to provide for ye two and ensure ye and she have a good life. If I'd kent—"

"If ye'd kent, ye'd have stayed out of duty. Ye'd have hated me and Maeve for it. Ye'll never be happy with a family. Yer way is lonely, remember?"

Aye, he'd said that. But even now, he didn't really believe in his own words. Being alone meant he wouldn't get hurt by losing someone he cared for and loved, like he'd lost Fiona. But it was too late now, he already cared for Deidre and for Maeve. And he'd never leave his child in danger of hunger and violence.

"I thought yer father would marry ye to someone who'd care for ye and would protect ye. That ye'd fake yer virginity or that he wouldn't notice. 'Tis quite another matter that ye turned out to be alone and rejected by yer own clan with a bairn to care for."

She crossed her arms on her chest. "I brought shame on my family. My father was disappointed in me. When I came and told my mother I was with child, she looked at me like I were a slug. The walls of Caerlaverock must still remember her scream." She went to sit on a bench by the wall of the kitchen. "Ye all taught me a valuable lesson nae to trust anyone but myself."

Hamish pinched the bridge of his nose. He'd broken her heart. He'd made her life miserable, and he was about to make it even worse. He'd agreed to kill his daughter's grandfather.

"Does she ken of her roots? Of her clan?"

"Nae. They dinna want to do anything with us."

So at least Maeve didn't know of her grandfather's existence. Deidre would be saddened, aye, but this was the father who'd left his daughter without protection on the streets.

Mayhap, Harris's death wouldn't be such a tragedy. Hamish would give the money Tailor paid him to Deidre.

His stomach ached. He watched her in wonder. Her blue eyes shone in the moonlight, the freckles on her nose like the stars above them. "How did ye survive all this time alone, lass?"

"Innis let me in, and I stayed with her for about two years. Deidre was born in that house. Then I started as a wet nurse, and we moved out. I was lucky to find employers who would let me bring Maeve."

Hamish studied her in wonder, taking in every detail of her face. Every eyelash, every freckle, every curve of her lips. The woman had the strength of iron within her. "Did ye say ye were a widow?"

"Aye. 'Twas the only way they'd let someone like me work in a good household. No one would take on a fallen woman with a bastart on her hands."

He sat next to her on the bench and took both her hands in his. They were so soft and delicate and small compared to his. She didn't snatch them out of his grasp, and the touch brought a warm wave of tingling through his arms. She looked up at him, her pupils widening and making her eyes indigo.

"I wilna let any harm come to ye nae more," he said. "I promise ye."

He leaned to her and kissed her. He expected defiance, a push, or another slap, but none came. Her lips welcomed him, surprising him with soft acceptance. He wrapped his arms around her waist and drew her closer to him. She smelled of milk, baked bread, and clean clothes, and her own feminine scent of herbs and flowers of a meadow. She bewitched him.

His body reacted instantly to her scent and the feel of her in his arms. His blood boiled, and his cock throbbed.

His heart drumming faster, his groin burning from desire, he picked her up and sat her on his lap, her legs on either side of his thighs. The kiss turned from gentle and appreciative into hungry and needy. He licked her tongue, sliding his over her delicious mouth, sucking on her lips. His hunger for her was urgent and hot.

God, he wanted her. The years apart fell away as though they had never happened. It was as though he held her for the first time in his arms, just like then, under the moon and starlight, a young lass, delicious and innocent and fiery.

And his...

He leaned back and took her face in both his hands, marveling at her. Her long eyelashes, the depths of her eyes, her soft lips. "Yer freckles are like those stars, only brown." Her eyes widened and shone, suddenly gaining more life and vibrancy.

"I've never stopped thinking of ye, lass," he said. "I havna loved anyone but ye. And now ye've given me the greatest gift. A bairn."

She released a small breath that left her mouth in a puff of steam.

"I will talk to Tailor on the morrow. Ye can give them a week's notice or until they find a new wet nurse. Ye wilna need for anything. We can go north, and ye can start a new life anywhere ye want with Maeve, somewhere new, where no one kens ye. Ye wilna need to work nae more—"

Her eyes flashed. "What?"

"I'll take care of ye and Maeve. Ye wilna need for anything."

She pushed off him and stood, her eyebrows arched, her mouth opened in disbelief.

"Ye want to take care of us after all these years? What

makes ye think I'll abandon everything and put my life and my daughter's life in yer hands? Ye *betrayed* me."

Hamish stood, too, stunned, hurt clawing at his heart. "Deidre, I wilna abandon ye nae more. I want to make this right."

"Oh, ye want to make this right? Will ye marry me, then?"

He frowned. "I didna mean marriage... I meant a cottage and an income... Mayhap a farm to manage."

He was no good for Deidre. There was no happiness in his future. Deidre could never love him after what he'd done to her.

"I wouldna force ye into a marriage ye dinna want."

"Oh, aye! I dinna want ye. Ye broke my heart once, and ye'll only break it again—or even worse, Maeve's. Dinna dare speak to her about this. Dinna come close to her again, and for everything that's holy, dinna say a word about ye being her da. If ye do, I wilna hesitate to take her and disappear from yer life so that ye wilna find me. Ye wilna betray me again."

Every word lashed at him like a whip. Regret crawled down his spine, leaving a burning trail.

"I can just kidnap ye and her and be done with it. Ye'll be safer with me than with the man who wants ye to be his mistress."

She raised her chin. "Ye just try. I still have my dagger with me, and I ken how to use it."

She turned on her heel and marched off, and he stared at her back and helplessly clenched and unclenched his fists. He wasn't afraid of her dagger, or her anger.

But he was afraid that if he did kidnap her, he'd lose any chance of her loving him.

Not that there was much hope of that anyway.

CHAPTER 8

December 23, 1308

The next day, Hamish stared at the empty goose nest in the stables as he waited for the warden. Was the gosling with his daughter?

His daughter...

Last night's revelation had left him restless. He moaned and turned in his bed at Innis's house. If Deidre thought she'd keep Maeve from him, she had another think coming. The more he thought about it, the more livid he got. She'd kept him in the dark about his child. And now that he had basically pressed the information out of her, she didn't want him to have anything to do with his own daughter. No doubt, she was ashamed of him. She was a laird's daughter, even if disinherited. He was an orphan, and the way he earned his coin wasn't something to be proud of. He didn't want Maeve to know what he did for a living.

And if John MacDougall sent someone after him again,

Deidre and Maeve could be in mortal danger. He couldn't do that to them. Whether that was a real risk or not, he didn't know. For now, as long as he breathed, he wouldn't let his daughter and the mother of his child be at the mercy of anyone, especially not a violent man like Tailor.

He had the means to force the warden to stop harassing Deidre.

Tailor came in the stables, large and imposing. "The Maxwells raided another village last night," he said without a greeting. "I'm getting fed up with all this nonsense."

He took out a dagger and handed it to Hamish, handle first.

"My man stole this from the Johnstone clan. Use it."

Hamish studied the dagger. The sigil was in silver on the hilt—a St. Andrew's cross with three golden rectangles. The blade was new, smooth, and sharp. Hamish's hands itched. How easy it would be to thrust this dagger right between the ribs of this huge boar and remove the threat to Deidre. He didn't want to use it on Deidre's father.

He would, but only if Tailor swore to leave Deidre alone.

"Aye." Hamish lowered his hand but didn't put the dagger in his belt. "But I do need to renegotiate the conditions of this job."

Tailor frowned, his eyes narrowing to two black dots. "Renegotiate?" His nostrils flared.

"Ye have a servant called Deidre."

Tailor's face went stone cold. "What about her?"

"I ken of yer wish to make her yer mistress. Ye will abandon that wish, and ye wilna touch her, or I wilna kill Harris Maxwell."

Tailor cocked one eyebrow, and the corner of his mouth rose in an amused half smile. "Are you seriously telling me what to do in my own household?"

Hamish's fingers clenched around the handle. "Ye will do as I say."

"Who is she to you?"

"It doesna matter."

"Oh, but it clearly does. She means something to you, does she?"

"That doesna concern ye."

He sighed and studied Hamish from under half-closed eyelids. "Is she your sister? A cousin, perhaps?" His eyes darkened. "Or did she lie when she said no man has touched her in nine years? Are you her lover?"

Hamish clenched his teeth tightly. Tailor crossed his arms on his chest, and his face turned into the vicious mask of a predator.

"She lives in my house. She nurses my child. I will do as I please with my women."

"She isna yer woman. And ye wilna touch her."

"Oh, I will touch her. In fact, if you don't accomplish the mission, she and her daughter will get the treatment of my whip."

Hamish's stomach churned, and horror crept through his blood like ice water. Deidre wouldn't leave here, and this man had her at his disposal—and not just her, but the wee Maeve as well.

He needed to be smart. He needed to eliminate Tailor. He didn't need the money as badly as he needed safety for the two lasses that mattered to him the most.

He wasn't going to kill Harris Maxwell. He was going to render Tailor harmless.

"Aye," Hamish said, his gut churning with rage. "I will accomplish yer mission. Just dinna hurt them. Agreed?"

A lazy, satisfied smile spread across Tailor's face. "Agreed."

Hamish hid the dagger and walked out of the stables. He needed to come clean to Deidre about everything, and ask for her help to protect their daughter.

~

It was around the midday meal when the door to the nursery opened and Deidre's head flew up. Stephen stopped nursing, startled by the noise. He unlatched and looked up at Deidre, a question in his wide eyes.

She lost her breath. Hamish stood in the doorway, his nostrils flaring, his fists clenched, his upper lip raised in a snarl.

Maeve stood up and came to sit by Deidre, and the gosling hobbled after her. She'd refused to leave the wee thing with the birds since he kept following her, and she'd agreed to clean after the thing thoroughly. Lady Matilda had said she didn't mind having him in the nursery if it remained clean enough.

Hamish's gaze fell on Deidre's naked breast, and the anger in his eyes changed to show an animallike need that made her inner muscles clench. Her mouth went dry as he marched into the room and stopped before her.

"Cover yerself, woman," he growled.

She closed her mouth and swallowed. Her legs felt heavy, and her breasts ached.

"Ye're nae supposed to be here." She hid her breast in the slit of her dress, stood, and put Stephen in his cot. "Go away, Hamish."

He glanced at Maeve, and his eyes warmed. "The gosling's doing well, lass, eh? Will ye be good and bring yer ma some water? I'm sure she's thirsty. And dinna hurry, aye?"

Maeve threw a quizzical glance at Deidre, who was already tired of Hamish's bossiness. She crossed her arms on her chest and opened her mouth to send him away yet again, but he interrupted.

"Deidre, I will talk to ye whether the lass is here or nae, and ye wilna want her to hear what I have to say."

The metal in his tone made her hair stand on end.

"Maeve, sweet, please do fetch me some water. And take the bowl with milk from the fireplace, please. I thank ye, lass."

Last night, Deidre had put milk out for the brownies, creatures that could help or ruin a household. Deidre liked to tell the children faerie tales and legends before they went to sleep. Since they now had the gosling, they could use the help of brownies to keep the nursery in order. Her grandmother from her mother's side came from the Highlands and had taught her to put milk near the fireplace overnight and make sure no man or beast drank from it.

"Aye, Ma." Maeve picked up her gosling and the bowl with milk. She threw a last, puzzled look at Hamish and then left the room, no doubt wondering why her mother insisted she didn't talk to Hamish while she was ready to stay in a room alone with him.

"Do be quick about it, Hamish," Deidre said once they were alone. "If anyone comes in and sees ye here..."

Hamish looked her up and down, and she felt as though a hot wave washed through her. "Were ye speaking the truth when ye said ye still have yer dagger?"

She frowned. "Aye. Why?"

"Have it on ye at all times."

She felt her face muscles go limp. "Why?"

"Because Tailor may harm ye. Or Maeve. And I canna be here to protect ye every moment of every day. So if ye dinna want to go with me, ye must do what I say."

She let out a sharp exhale and nodded. "How do ye ken that?"

"Because he just told me. So I need yer help, Deidre. I want to get rid of him once and for all."

She paled. "Kill him?"

"Nae. Not necessarily."

"Then what?"

He inhaled. "Ye must ken the truth first. I ken ye hate me already, so ye canna hate me even more."

Something about his tone brought a chill to her. "What?"

"He hired me to kill yer da."

Oh, he didn't think she could hate him more? "Ye pig," she spat.

"I didna kill him yet, and I wilna."

"Oh, ye wilna?" She moved to one of her chests, rummaged through it, and procured her father's dagger. She pointed it at his throat. "Of course ye wilna. I wilna let ye."

He studied her. "Ye dinna wish yer father ill after what he did to ye?"

Her hand shook, and she tensed it to make it stop, but it only trembled more. "Of course I dinna wish him ill. He's my da."

Hamish took the blade between his index finger and thumb and set it to the side. She dropped her hand and let the dagger hang alongside her body. He cupped her face, and his hand was callused, warm, and scratchy.

"Yer da has been raiding Tailor's villages in secret. Tailor's men figured it out. In the twelve days of Christmas, there will be a peace between the Marches, and the wardens must strictly obey it, making sure there's nae raiding."

Her da was a reiver... A spasm constricted Deidre's throat. She had heard the English had taken Caerlaverock, but she hadn't thought it was that bad. They must really be in trouble if her da had lowered himself to reiving.

"Have ye seen him?"

"Aye. 'Tis nae good, Deidre. I wilna lie to ye. Caerlaverock was damaged in the wars against the Bruce. They are struggling."

They were struggling... Worry churned her gut. "And my ma?"

"I've seen her, too. Yer sisters are marrit and nae longer live at home."

"Oh." Of course they were. They'd always been good lasses, true women who did what women were supposed to do—marry well and take care of the household. "Good. I'm glad."

"So I have a plan to take Tailor down and make him leave. But I need yer and yer da's help for that. What do ye say? We do this together. For ye. For Maeve."

Working together with him to take down Tailor? Was she ready to trust him in that way? There was a time when she'd say aye without a moment of hesitation. That was before he'd left her.

"For me? For Maeve?" she said. "We're perfectly fine where we are."

"Ye're wrong, Deidre. I ken he wants ye to be his mistress, and I told him to leave ye alone. He's a violent man. I'm sure ye ken."

Hamish was right. Tailor was dangerous. But so far, he hadn't posed any threat to her or, God forbid, to her daughter.

"He didna do anything to us."

"Nae yet. But he will. He told me so."

She gasped. "What?"

"Aye. When I told him to leave ye alone, he threatened to flog ye. And worse. Maeve."

A sick, violent man like Tailor was capable of something like that. If Hamish was right about Tailor, and he was a threat to her or Maeve, she had two choices. She could either run or work with Hamish to take him down.

Where would she run to? Here, she had friends. She knew people. If she ran, she would be a woman alone with a child, with no protection, no connections, and no money. They'd need to start from scratch. And Deidre couldn't put her daughter through more years of a poor, hungry existence.

Teaming up with Hamish was better than taking him up on his offer to take care of Maeve and her. That way she would still have her independence, and she would keep her reputation intact. She could go and get hired by another family.

If they worked together, she'd need to be very careful. She could not trust his promises and not let him get too close to Maeve.

"Aye. Let's take the bastart down. What do ye have in mind?"

"The only one who has power over Tailor is the bishop of

Carlisle. Tomorrow is Christmas Eve, and the peace treaty starts. He will visit Tailor and will be verra angry if there is any raiding during those twelve days of Christmas." Hamish took out the Johnstone's dagger. "So we use Tailor's own plan against him."

CHAPTER 9

Later that day, Deidre's heart hammered hard against her rib cage as she stepped soundlessly into the dark hall towards the lord and lady's chamber. Hamish walked behind her, as quiet as a cat. Aye, they had their differences. Aye, she was furious at him. And, aye, she was afraid he'd break her heart and abandon her and Maeve again.

Despite all that, just for this moment, it felt amazing to be able to rely on him. To have his hard, stable shoulder to lean on. To know that he had her back, even if temporarily.

Mayhap he wasn't the man for her in the long term, but without a shadow of a doubt, she knew he would protect her and Maeve until his dying breath if need be.

And after nine years of struggling to survive, of constant fear and loneliness, his protection was like a breath of fresh air.

They had to be very careful. If she was noticed in the lord and lady's chamber, she'd be let go without any pay. If Hamish was spotted, he would be arrested. Since Tailor was the one who gave out justice, he'd no doubt have Hamish beheaded.

But they needed to act, and they needed to act now.

Deidre opened the door a little to peer inside the chamber. She heard voices...

"They're inside," she whispered to Hamish. "We must back up."

"You ungrateful woman!" She heard Tailor's booming voice. "You stupid, stupid woman. How many times have I told you to have my clothes cleaned every day?"

There was a hard slap and a female yelp. Deidre looked at Hamish, whose face darkened.

"Hamish," she whispered hotly. "Please, dinna snap. I beg of ye. 'Tisna time now."

His hand that lay on the wall clenched into a fist. "I ken, Deidre. I wilna."

Heavy steps boomed towards them, and they sneaked into an alcove where the light didn't reach. Deidre heard the door *swoosh* open, and Tailor's large figure walked past them. Deidre only now noticed that Hamish had pressed her against the wall, his hands on both sides of her face, shielding her completely from Tailor or anyone passing by. His face hung over hers, handsome and dark, and there was a longing in his black eyes. She could just reach up an inch and kiss him, plunge into his delicious taste...

It felt like the air had been sucked out of the hall, and heat rushed through her core. For nine years, no man had touched her. For nine years, she'd longed for him, dreamed of him claiming her again and again, and now here he was.

The sound of steps interrupted her thoughts, and she looked to the side. Lady Matilda passed by. She'd put on a wimple that covered her neck and ears, and a veil that fell over her shoulders with a band on her head. Poor woman. She slouched forward and held her stomach and she went into the nursery down the hall.

Deidre and Hamish's eyes locked.

"I do like being snuggled with ye so, lass," he whispered. "But let's go."

They sneaked into the bedchamber. The room was large and had a massive wooden bed with a canopy suspended over it. A carved poster stood at each corner with red curtains gathered around it, and two windows with brown horn sheets let yellow daylight in. Fire burned in the fireplace, making the room warm and cozy. Carved chests stood along the length of the wall, as well as a closet with beautifully carved flowers and leaves on it. Deidre's heart ached. She hadn't seen good furniture like that for nine years. She'd had a gorgeous carved bed back in Caerlaverock. She'd forgotten how nice it was to be surrounded by expensive things.

That didn't matter now. She led Hamish to the door on the opposite side of the room. On the other side of the door was a small room decorated with shields, swords, and maces. There, next to a single window, was what they were looking for—Tailor's suit of armor, specially made for his size.

Hamish retrieved the burlap sack he had tucked under his cloak. "Let's get to work."

They retrieved the helm with Tailor's coat of arms on it—one diagonal line with two keys on either side of it. They took the breastplate, the neck and shoulder pieces, the arm and leg harnesses. They worked fast, but time crawled by, and they froze at every rustle and noise.

Finally, everything was in the sack, and Hamish grunted as he put it over his shoulder.

"Go check the hall, lass," Hamish said.

"Aye." She walked through the bedchamber to the door and peered through the slit. It was dark and empty. "'Tis clear."

Hamish walked to the door. "If he notices the armor is missing, he'll get angry and be suspicious. He may send people to investigate. Go now somewhere where people can see ye. Like the kitchen."

"Aye."

"Ye ken what to do. We act tomorrow, on Christmas Eve."

Deidre swallowed hard at the thought of what she'd need

to do to get Tailor to disappear for the night. But Hamish didn't need to know what she had in mind.

"Aye. I'll do my part, Hamish. Now go to my family."

HAMISH'S HORSE WAS EXHAUSTED BY THE TIME HE REACHED Caerlaverock later that day. It had taken half of the afternoon to get there. Thankfully, it hadn't snowed, and the ground was frozen solid, making Hamish's way quick.

"Lord Maxwell," he called to one of the guards as he rode inside the castle. "Where's Lord Maxwell? I must speak to him now."

Harris ran down from the tower, his face worried. "Hamish? What is it?"

"Can we talk without other ears listening," he said, throwing a sideways glance at the English warriors standing on the wall watching them.

"Aye." Harris led him into the kitchens where a cook was lazily kneading dough for bread. They went into a larder where smoked meat hung, as well as dried, salted fish. "What happened?"

Hamish retrieved the Johnstone dagger and held it out for Harris to see. "George Tailor hired me to kill ye with this on Christmas Day."

Harris's face went blank at first, then his eyebrows knit together, and his icy-blue eyes darkened, just like Deidre's when she was angry. "Ye were going to kill me?"

Despite his age, Harris unsheathed his sword with a lightning-fast movement, but Hamish was faster and deflected the sword with the Johnstone dagger, placing the edge of the blade against Harris's throat.

"I was," Hamish said, "but I'm nae anymore. Unless ye make the wrong move now."

Harris stared at him, his upper lip curled up into a snarl.

"I came here to save yer life," Hamish said. "So toss yer sword on the ground."

Harris did that, and the metal clunked against the stone.

"Now I'm going to step back and put away the dagger, and we'll talk about it calmly, aye?"

Harris eyed him, unconvinced. "Aye."

Hamish stepped back. "Ye chased Deidre away, pregnant and alone."

Harris's face fell. "How do ye ken?"

"She works for him. She's a wet nurse for his bairn."

Harris's eyes watered. "Is she well?"

"She is. Only thanks to her strong will and determination. Yer granddaughter is well, too."

"Granddaughter?"

"Aye. Maeve. She has Deidre's freckles."

Harris closed his eyes and pinched the bridge of his nose, shaking his head. "I canna believe I did that to her...chased her away to save the great name and honor of the Maxwell clan. And look at us now. Where's the glory? Where's the pride? Why did I sacrifice my daughter for something the English could just take anyway?"

Hamish sighed. "Well, if ye want to rectify yer deeds, ye have a way. Tailor's threatened her and Maeve if I dinna kill ye. But I had enough of his cruelty. He beats his wife. He beats his servants. He's a dangerous man, and I've seen my share of those. Deidre is fighting for ye in Carlisle now, in Tailor's house. Will ye fight for her here?"

Harris raised his chin. "Aye. Of course I will."

Hamish nodded. "Good. We will need a dozen or so of yer most trusted men. And nae a word to the Sassenachs that garrison in yer castle. Tomorrow is Christmas Eve. Do ye have a large, tall man in yer clan? And a village somewhere on yer lands that is so loyal to ye they would lie to a bishop?"

CHAPTER 10

December 24, 1308

Christmas Eve in the Tailor household arrived with a loud awakening. Somewhere deep in the house, a man roared like a bear. The lord must be awake and angry at the lady for some reason.

Last night, Deidre had seen Tailor ogling her with his lustful, hungry eyes as she passed him in the courtyard. In the evening, he got very drunk and passed out, as he often did. Deidre knew he would take out his sore head on his poor wife, and she didn't look forward to his wrath. A worm of guilt moved in Deidre's gut. Would Lady Matilda have to take a beating because of Hamish and her?

The door to the nursery opened, and Lady Matilda rushed in, closed the door shut behind her, and leaned against it. She was in her shift, her hair was still in disarray, and her eyes were wide.

"Where is my uisge?" boomed Tailor's voice from behind the door as he passed by.

Alice and Lucia woke up, too.

"Mother, what's wrong?" Alice said, sitting up.

Matilda came to sit on the bed and hugged Alice, and Lucia joined, laying her head on her mother's lap.

"Nothing, dear," Matilda said. "I came to wish you a good Christmas Eve. We go to Mass later and will give alms to the poor, so I just want to make sure you two are bathed and combed and look your best."

She looked at Deidre. "The lord seems to be out of sorts this morning."

Deidre hugged Maeve, who was waking up.

"How odd," Deidre said. "Mayhap faeries took his uisge?"

Matilda chuckled. "You Scots have the strangest beliefs."

"Aye. Well, some believe faeries bring people prosperity and good health in exchange for teeth. Others even believe faeries can take people through time to find love."

Matilda shook her head. "Please, stop. Don't put those pagan stories into the girls' heads." She looked at her daughters. "There aren't any faeries. No time travel. And no health in exchange for teeth. There's only our Lord Jesus Christ, and his birthday is tomorrow. That's what we celebrate." She scowled at Deidre. "Will you help me get them ready?"

Deidre stood up. If she did her part right, she wouldn't be with this family for long; though, she'd miss Stephen and the lasses.

"Aye, my lady."

"The bishop will come tomorrow to dine with us on Christmas Day," she said to the girls, who stood up from the bed and began changing for their bath. "He'll bless us for the year to come, and we'll have a roasted goose."

Maeve gave a small squeak, and Deidre squeezed her hand to reassure her and keep her quiet.

"Aye, my lady. I'll feed Stephen."

The day passed quickly with preparations for the holiday. Servants cleaned the house, and branches of holly were hung. Their thick green leaves were beautiful, and the red berries shone and reflected the light of the torches and fireplaces. Work in the kitchen was in full swing, and the courtyard smelled deliciously of fresh meat pies.

Deidre's stomach squeezed. Ever since her father chased her away, she'd been sad at Christmas. She missed her family. She missed her father, her mother, and her sisters. She missed sitting all together and celebrating the birth of their Lord Jesus Christ.

Later that evening, the Tailors and most of the household went to Mass held in the church that the bishop of Carlisle himself led. Latin words fell on the crowd like rain. No one understood anything, but everyone listened and prayed. Tailor threw lustful gazes at Deidre across the aisle that separated men and women. This time, Deidre didn't look away, even though his gazes brought bile up from her stomach. She bounced fussy Stephen on her hip and stared back at Tailor.

Good, ye bastart, she thought. The weight of Hamish's small glass bottle in her pocket was palpable. *Ogle me all ye like. I have something coming for ye.*

Hamish had given her the bottle before he left with the armor and instructed her on how to use its contents. Her stomach churned with worry. Had Hamish been successful in Caerlaverock? Or was she going to put herself in danger for nothing?

On the way home, Tailor lingered a bit behind. Lady Matilda took sleepy Stephen, and she and the girls went to the nursery. Maeve went to check on Maccus in the pen.

"My lord," Deidre said, and Tailor turned to her.

"Deidre." He stepped closer, until his stomach almost touched her. "Something you want to tell me?"

"I do." Deidre forced herself to stay in place and not step back. "Might we speak in private? Mayhap in the stables?"

"In the stables?" He looked her up and down, a triumphant smile on his face. "My, my. Of course we may, dear."

Part of her hated herself for doing this. She wasn't this woman, a seductress and a liar.

For Maeve, she thought. *For Maeve and my father.*

He let her pass, and once they were in the stables, she bravely went to an empty stall with fresh hay. She went all the way inside the stall. She wouldn't be able to drag his massive body and cover him with hay, so she needed him to drop there.

It was almost completely dark in the stall, and it smelled comfortingly like horses, and manure, and hay.

She turned to face Tailor. He stood completely still before her.

"Tell me," he said, his voice deep and slow with lust. "What is it? Though, I think I know."

Deidre inhaled a lungful of air for bravery. "I've thought about yer proposal."

"And?"

"I will become yer mistress, my lord."

He gave a low, long growl of triumph. "Come here, you hot Scottish wildling. I'll show you what you've been missing all these years." He stepped towards her, but she put her hands on his chest to stop him.

"My lord, please. Might we have a drink before? As ye said, I havna been with a man for a long time."

"Well, of course. Go and fetch something."

"I already have it here. I thought ye might enjoy a drink since I ken how much ye like it."

"Hmm, how thoughtful of you, Deidre." She retrieved a skin of uisge. She'd sent a man to one of the Scottish villages on the border to buy it and poured some in the skin from the storage room. She'd also brought two cups.

She turned her back to him and poured the drink in his cup. With a shaky hand, she uncorked the small, cold bottle and turned it over. As Hamish's potion connected with the uisge, it gurgled, and her heart raced. Had Tailor noticed anything? She had no idea what was in the potion, but Hamish had told her he often used it on missions, and it would make Tailor drop into a deep sleep. She added a splash of uisge in her own cup.

She turned back to Tailor and handed it to him. He took it with a sly smile on his face. He didn't seem to suspect anything.

"Sláinte," she said, and they touched the cups.

He downed the contents and grunted, seemingly satisfied. Deidre poured more uisge into his cup. The man was so huge, he probably needed a couple of waterskins to fall unconscious. He threw back the contents in one gulp, took her by the waist, and drew her to him. The faint smell of stale male sweat touched her nostrils.

"More, my lord?" she said, wriggling out of his grasp. "I certainly need more."

She added more uisge to his vessel and sipped hers. She needed more bravery to deal with him. Her heart pounded, and her cold hands trembled. What if the potion didn't work on him? What if there was too little of it for his body?

"Last one, love," he said. "I'm already burning for you. I'll melt all your reservations away."

Nausea rose in her stomach at the thought of his naked body crushing hers. *Please, potion, work... Please...*

"Aye, my lord. Last one."

She filled the cup to the brim, and some of the uisge spilled. This was the last of it. He drank it in three gulps and threw the cup into the hay.

"Now, come here, love." He started to slur his consonants.

Good, maybe it was working. She just needed to wait a bit.

She gulped her own drink and it reminded her of Da's uisge... Mayhap, it was?

Jesu, give me strength.

Tailor stepped towards her, wrapped his arms around her

waist, and crushed her to his large body. She didn't even have the time to react. He put his hand on the back of her head and pressed his mouth to hers.

The smell of alcohol mixed with his own scent of stale food and old sweat invaded her senses. His mouth was hard and demanding, and he licked her closed lips with his tongue like a cow. She froze in his embrace, fighting with all the willpower she had not to push him back, not to anger him. She tensed her shoulders until they ached and shut her eyes.

He let her go. "Come, love, loosen up." His consonants were even more slurred now, but he was still as strong as a bull. "Give me your sweet, sweet mouth..."

He pressed her to himself again, his rough hands kneading her so hard, her ribs hurt. She couldn't stand it. She itched to reach for her dagger and gut him like a fish.

No, she couldn't rely on Hamish's potion anymore. She had to do something.

She pushed herself away, gulping for fresh air, but he grasped her hand, grunting and impatient like a toddler. God, give her patience...

"Wait," she said. "Wait, my lord..."

She sank to her knees, desperately searching in the hay around her. If Hamish's potion wouldn't do the job, she had to take matters in her own hands. Straw prickled her fingers, but she couldn't find what she was looking for.

"What are you doing, love?"

"I want to please ye." She grunted as she reached farther into the hay.

"I will please you..."

He collapsed on top of her, knocking all the breath out of her lungs. She gasped, unable to inhale. He shut her mouth with his, invading her with his thick tongue, and making her gag. She clawed at him, but it only spurred his lust, and he moaned. He'd squish her like a boulder on an ant. She searched with her hand, trying to reach the dagger, but she must be lying right on it. With her other hand, she felt about until she touched something hard. She stretched out, reaching for it. She strained for the piece of wood. Her fingers scratched the surface of the wood once...twice... The air was disappearing from her lungs, and spots flashed before her eyes. Her chest hurt, and her ribs felt like they were about to crack.

She lurched towards the wood and grasped it. With the last strength that she had, she swung the wood and hit Tailor with it on the back of his head.

He grunted, stilled, and went limp on top of her.

She moaned and pushed him off her, but he didn't budge. Surprisingly, it felt like he weighed less now that he was completely immobile. She wriggled and turned and managed to roll out from under him.

She grabbed her dagger, just in case, and pointed it at him, but he didn't move. She poked him with the tip of her foot. Nothing.

She felt for the pulse at his neck—it beat.

Finally, she allowed herself a deep sigh of relief. The combination of uisge and Hamish's potion had not been enough, but the blow to the head had finally done it.

She gathered some hay and covered him with it so that no one would see him at first glance.

She could only hope he'd stay asleep for the whole night.

And that Hamish's plan would work in Caerlaverock.

CHAPTER 11

The Christmas Eve Mass had just finished when Hamish, Harris, and his eleven men arrived at the village of Auchlyne. Snow glowed white on the ground and on the thatched roofs against the black sky. Unsuspecting villagers were on their way to their homes from the only stone building in the village—a wee church. Only the village chief and a few trusted men knew what was about to happen. It was important to make the farce appear real so the people believed they were being raided.

Harris, Hamish, and the rest wore English helms and brandished English shields and swords that they'd "kindly borrowed" from the garrison in Caerlaverock. The lower halves of their faces were covered with pieces of cloth to make sure the villagers wouldn't recognize them as Maxwell men. Their biggest asset—literally their biggest asset—was Wyatt, the largest man of the Maxwell clan. And he was still too skinny for the armor. The men had stuffed pillows under it so that he'd fill it up.

The helm shielded his face, so no one would know it wasn't Tailor himself. Not that anyone in the village would recognize

Tailor. Auchlyne lay on the border with England, so it was realistic for the English to ride there from Carlisle.

Hamish spotted the chief of the village. He held a torch and walked with his wife, surrounded by their children. Only he and several other of the most trusted villagers knew about the plan.

Hamish looked at Harris, who nodded to him.

"Let's go, lads," Harris said. "Begin, Wyatt."

Wyatt whistled, drawing the attention of the villagers. They looked stunned. Hamish and the Maxwells spurred their horses and launched at them.

"Reivers!" cried Neachdainn, the village chief. "Run! Give them anything they want and dinna fight them!"

The villagers screamed, yelled, and ran in every direction. The Maxwells galloped into the village, waving their swords. They rode right through the people, careful not to hurt anyone. They kicked barrels and set a haystack on fire. It had been specifically laid separate from the buildings to make sure nothing else would burn. They dismounted and went inside the houses, demanding furs, silver, clothes, and food.

They broke things, they tore things, they spilled things. They slapped and hit the men who were especially antagonistic, but they didn't cause actual harm. They took sheep and cows and horses. In the end, as agreed, the village chief dragged Wyatt down from his horse and they made a very public show of fighting each other with swords. At the end of the fight, the chief dragged Wyatt's helm off his head. After that, the Maxwells fought their way to Wyatt and pushed their leader back up onto his horse, leaving the helm behind.

Driving the cattle ahead of them, they rode off into the night.

They hid the cows on an abandoned farm, where Hamish changed into a peasant's clothes. They peeled the suit of armor off Wyatt, put it in a sack, and put the sack on a cart full of firewood. Hamish clicked his tongue, and the horse pulling the cart started south.

They left everything they'd raided on the abandoned farm. Later on, everything will be returned to the villagers, as agreed with the chief.

Hamish arrived at the warden's house in the dark, although the sky was starting to lighten on the horizon. The gates were closed, and everything was completely dark and quiet behind the stone walls. Was Deidre all right? Had she managed to pour the sleeping potion into Tailor's drink? The bastart would rather die than pass on a stiff uisge, although Hamish hated the idea of Deidre being close enough to slip it into his drink.

"Anyone awake?" he called out in a Cumbrian accent.

No one answered. The guards, like the rest of the people, might have fallen asleep after Christmas Eve dinner, lulled by good food and more alcohol than necessary.

"Hello!"

The door of the gate opened, and a sleepy guard peeked from behind it, rubbing his eyes. "Who goes there?"

"'Tis me, ol' Berwick. I brought firewood."

"Who?" The guard scratched his beard.

"Berwick. Firewood. 'Tis Christmas Day, Lady Matilda ordered more firewood."

"Oh... It's still night."

"'Tis already mornin'. Take yer head out of yer arse. The sun is about to rise."

The guard glanced at the brightening sky, sighed, and pushed the gate open. "Good man," Hamish said as he passed him on the cart.

"But dinna expect me to help," the guard said.

"Go back to sleep," Hamish muttered to himself.

He stopped the cart by the stables and began unloading firewood on the pile that leaned against the kitchen wall. He glanced at the guard from time to time, and soon the man went back inside a small shack. He would probably doze off again. Hamish didn't think he suspected anything.

Most of the household was asleep, but smoke rose from the kitchen chimney. The cooks were already up and preparing pies and roasting geese. The bishop would arrive around midday for the Christmas feast. Branches of holly with bright-red berries decorated every house and workshop.

Hamish wondered what it was like to celebrate Christmas with a family, what it would be like to celebrate with Deidre and Maeve... Would he ever be able to let go of the cold barrier around his soul? Would he ever be able to allow himself to commit to a woman for a lifetime?

Not just any woman.

Deidre. Deidre and his daughter.

He imagined the three of them sitting at a table with a wreath of holly, meat pies, and a roasted goose. Fire playing cheerfully in the fireplace. Deidre smiling to him across the table, their hands intertwined. Maeve next to him, chirping about her gosling, Maccus, and what they'd done today...

The image in his head turned black, burning to ash. Because life would take them away from him—an illness, an enemy, or just bad luck. Just like Fiona had been taken. The thought brought a wave of icy-cold terror through his veins.

No. They were better off without him. Deidre would never forgive him anyway. All he could do was to eliminate the threat of George Tailor and set her free. He'd continue being a mercenary and send money to her whether she wanted to or not, because there was no way he'd let his child starve or be put in danger if he could help it.

He went inside the stables. The horses snorted peacefully. He took a torch and checked all the stalls. The farthest stall to the left had no horse in it. He went there and held the torch up. There, in the heap of hay, he saw a hand.

He sighed with relief. Tailor was here. Hamish went back to the cart and took the sack with the armor. He carried it into the stall and threw it in the hay next to Tailor. He itched to find Deidre and talk to her, tell her the good news, that the pretend raid had gone well and no one had gotten hurt. The villagers must be on their way here now to proclaim the treaty had been broken and demand reconciliation.

He went back to the cart and unloaded the rest of the firewood, then woke the guard again, and disappeared behind the gates.

CHAPTER 12

December 25, 1308

"Bless you, Lady Matilda," Bishop William of Carlisle said.

Deidre bounced the wee Stephen on her hip. Maeve stood next to her. The Tailor family, all except for the lord of the house, stood in a line in the courtyard and smiled as the bishop made the sign of cross over the lady of the house. She kissed the ring on his finger.

The bishop wore a long, white dalmatic with an intricate pattern sewn in golden-and-silver threads. A cross hung from his neck, and he held a crozier in his right hand. The staff was decorated with many carved ornaments. The head was large and round and had the most delicate carving of Mary, Joseph, and baby Jesus. The bishop was a short man with a full gray beard and cold gray eyes.

Was he someone who cared more about the well-being of

people? Or was he a politician who would be more concerned with staying in the good graces of the warden?

Their whole plan was based on the assumption that the bishop would abhor violence committed on the holy Christmas Eve, especially when there was a truce between the Scottish and the English Marches.

But what if he didn't care about that? What if he remained the warden's ally through and through?

Deidre's heart drummed against her rib cage. She didn't have time to go and check on the warden and see if Hamish had delivered the armor. But Tailor was nowhere to be seen. If he'd come back to his bedchamber, Lady Matilda would have brought him here. The worried, stern look on Lady Matilda's face told Deidre the woman had no knowledge of her husband's whereabouts.

Mayhap it would all work out. Mayhap they had a chance.

"And where's the noble lord himself?" the bishop asked.

"Indisposed, my lord bishop. I'm afraid he's ill."

Or mayhap he had returned to his bedchamber and she just hadn't been able to wake him up?

"What ails him?" the bishop asked.

"Illness of the bowels, my lord bishop."

A small grimace of concern crossed his features. "Perhaps I should go and bless him?"

She inhaled sharply. "No, my lord bishop... That is, I thank you, but I wouldn't want to offend your senses on this holy day."

His eyes grew stony. "I have been a simple priest, Lady Matilda. I have seen and treated all kinds of pestilences and sicknesses."

She gave a crooked nod of resignation. "Of course."

"We must hold West English March together, he and I. I do have high hopes he will be able to finally bestow peace upon these godforsaken lands and protect simple people against the barbarian Scots."

"I do not know much about those things, but I'm sure that is exactly his wish."

"Stop! Who goes there?" a call came from the guard who stood by the open gates.

Deidre bit her lip, her stomach squeezing.

"We must speak to the bishop," said someone from outside.

The guard darted to close the gate, but several riders rode past him. There were six of them. Her heart gave a lurch as she saw Hamish. He was clearly exhausted. There were dark shadows under his eyes, but they shone brightly when he looked at her. He gave her a barely noticeable nod, and her knees went weak. It was just like the first moment they'd met, when he'd ridden into Caerlaverock and stolen her breath away.

She tore her gaze from Hamish and saw who rode the horse next to him. Her stomach dropped as the man stared straight at her, his face distorted in a grimace of pain and love.

Her father.

He dismounted the horse, and her eyes blurred with tears.

He'd aged. Gone was the man she'd considered the strongest and most powerful lord in the world. Gone was the proud, mighty overlord. An old man stood before her, wrinkled and slouched. His long hair and beard were gray and silver. A damned tear ran down her cheek.

"I am the bishop of Carlisle. What is this about?"

Her father cleared his throat and looked at the bishop. "My lord bishop. I am the warden of Scottish West March, and I've come to seek justice."

"From me?"

"Aye. Last night, on a holy night, the warden of West English March attacked and raided the village of Auchlyne on my lands." He lifted Tailor's helm and held it high. "The man lost this at the raid, and Neachdainn, the chief of Auchlyne, brought it to me. Since 'tis a peace treaty between our two

Marches for the twelve days of Christmas, and he broke it, I've come so ye can resolve this and punish yer warden's violent actions."

Lady Matilda came and took baby Stephen from Deidre's hands. Her eyes were wide, her face pale. Deidre squeezed Maeve's hand, her pulse beating hard against her temples. What would the bishop say? Would he believe them? If he did, would he do anything?

"Who is Neachdainn?" Bishop said.

"I am." A man came forward. He had a wild, bushy beard and curly gray hair under his dirty cap. He had the stern look of defiance and stubbornness of a true Scot. He stood with his legs wide apart and crossed his arms on his chest.

The bishop came a few steps towards him, narrowing his cold eyes. "Is this true?"

"Aye. Every word. I fought the lord myself. My men will confirm that, too. Look at the cuts and bruises." He turned his head to his three men. One of them had a black eye, the other's arm was suspended in a sling. The third one had a blood-caked bandage around his head. "My people lost sheep, cows, clothes, seed, coin, and utensils. I demand justice. 'Tis a grave sin to raid on the holy night."

"This cannot be true." The bishop looked at Lady Matilda. "He couldn't have gone to Auchlyne last night because he's ill, isn't he?"

Lady Matilda paled even more. Her eyelashes fluttered, and she bowed her head. "I have sinned, my lord bishop. I lied to you. Please, forgive me. He isn't ill. He isn't in his bed. I don't know where he is."

The bishop's lips flattened in a single line. "But he was at the mass last night."

"The raid happened late at night," her father said. "'Tis likely he went after the mass."

The bishop looked at Matilda. "This doesn't make sense. Why would he do that? Is there a reason, Lady Matilda?"

She looked down at her feet, sobbed, and nodded. "We barely have any silver left."

The bishop's jaw tightened, and he inhaled sharply. "It does sound like a grave offense against our Lord Jesus Christ. I must speak to the warden himself. We must find him or wait until he appears. But if all this is true..." He shook his head. "I must write to the king and ask for him to appoint a new warden. This post is about upholding justice and making sure there is an end to the raiding. If the warden wants to become a reiver himself, he cannot stay here."

Lady Matilda continued sobbing and pressed wee Stephen against herself tighter. He began wailing, too, reaching his arms to Deidre. Poor wee thing. He'd need to get used to another wet nurse soon.

Deidre's and Hamish's eyes locked together from across the courtyard. His were triumphant. She suppressed a longing to run to him and revel in the safety of his warm, strong arms.

"What is the meaning of this?" boomed a loud voice.

Deidre turned her head towards the stables. Tailor leaned against the doorframe, straw clinging to his hair and clothes. He looked like he could barely hold his head up. One hand was pressed against the side of his head, where Deidre had hit him. He looked like death. His eyes were bloodshot, his eye sockets dark and sunken. He was ashen.

"Warden," the bishop said. "Did you sleep in the stables?"

"It's certainly where I woke up," Tailor said.

"Did you or did you not raid the village of Auchlyne on Scottish West March last night after the holy Mass?"

Tailor squinted, looking puzzled. "What?"

"Did you raid these men's village?" He pointed at Harris and Neachdainn.

Tailor looked at Harris, then at Hamish standing near him, and his face grew livid. "I did not."

"These men claim that you did, and they have proof—your helm. Where's the rest of your armor?"

He paled. "Does not matter where it is. I did not raid anything. She can prove it." He stabbed his finger at Deidre. "She was with me last night after the mass. She seduced me, got me drunk with uisge. Tell them, you bloody Scotswoman."

Deidre raised her chin. "The lord has made unwanted advances at me, but I certainly didna agree to them."

The bishop narrowed his eyes at Tailor. "Does your head ail you, my lord?"

"She hit me with something!" Tailor growled.

"I hit him, my lord bishop," said Neachdainn. "We fought, I got a grasp of his helm and hit him with a branch. The lord came at me with his sword. I had to protect myself."

The bishop sighed. "Where is the rest of your armor, Lord Tailor?"

He sulked at the bishop. "Do not believe these lies, my lord bishop!"

"Where. Is. It?"

"Mayhap 'tis where he just came from?" Harris said. "The stables."

The bishop marched towards the stables, his staff thumping softly against the snowy ground. Harris, Hamish, and Neachdainn followed him. Tailor helplessly let them pass in. Poor Stephen kept wailing. Deidre bit her lip, the motherly instinct to reach out and take the poor wee babe and soothe him itching her arms.

After some time, the bishop and the rest came out of the stables.

"You broke the peace treaty between the Marches," he said, mournfully. "But what's even worse, you broke the sacred peace of the holy night before Christmas. The king will hear of this, and because of your grave misdeed, you will be relieved of your post. You must leave here, my lord. This was a non-Christian act. The warden of Western March cannot be one who breaks his own laws."

Relief ran through Deidre, and a grin she couldn't contain

spread across her face. Her father would be all right. She and Maeve were out of danger. Hamish hadn't betrayed her trust, and his plan had worked. Finally, something good had happened.

And thank the Lord, it had happened on Christmas.

CHAPTER 13

"Deidre," Harris said. "Might we talk?"

The courtyard was almost empty. The bishop and Tailor had gone into the great hall to discuss the matter of him losing his post. Lady Matilda and her children had gone back to the nursery. Maeve stood by Deidre and stared at Harris with curiosity. Hamish, Neachdainn, and his men waited by the gate. The guard threw wary glances at them.

Deidre licked her lips. Her stomach was turning and twisting. Anger at her father that she'd held back all these years came to the surface and seethed in her veins. It mixed with a sadness she didn't understand as well as elation to see him well and alive. The last time she'd seen him, he'd been red-faced and pointing at the door, screaming for her to get out, to not shame the good Maxwell name.

She glanced at Maeve. "Wait for me here, sweet, aye?"

"I'll go check on Maccus."

"Aye."

Deidre approached Harris. His icy-blue eyes were duller now, the whites around his pupils yellower. There were deep wrinkles around his eyes, and bags under them.

"Maccus?" he said.

"'Tis a gosling that follows her."

"Does she ken?"

She shook her head once. "Nae. She doesna ken about clan Maxwell. 'Tis a coincidence she called her gosling so."

"Mayhap she felt something in her blood. The call of her bloodline."

Deidre crossed her arms on her chest. "The bloodline that her verra existence shamed."

Harris took a deep breath and sighed. "I was a fool, lass. I was angry and hurt. Ye ken how stubborn I am. Through the years, I've come to realize I made a mistake chasing ye away."

Deidre's eyes filled with tears. Her chest ached as though cats scratched it. "Oh?"

"I've missed ye. Ye're my fiery lass, my sweet warrior, the only one who wanted to train with swords and ride horses with me. I suppose because ye were my favorite, I was so hurt and disappointed in ye. I was terrified of what I'd done by putting those independent ideas in yer head. I wasna able to protect ye from the man who took advantage of ye."

"No one took advantage of me, Da," she said with her head held high. "They were all my decisions and my actions. I'm responsible for my own deeds."

"My strong lass..." His voice rasped, broken. "Will ye please come back home?"

The words opened something within her, and a cascade of feelings flooded her chest. Relief, elation, love. She hurt, but it was the pain of a wound being cleaned of dirt, a wound on the mend.

But could she trust her father again after his betrayal?

"I'm nae ready to forgive ye, Da. Do ye understand what ye did to my life and Maeve's? Do ye realize what we've been through? Hunger, cold, sickness. She almost died of a cough when she was a bairn."

Harris shut his eyes, wrinkling his face. "I'm sorry, lass. I'm so sorry. Please, will ye forgive me? Will ye let me care for ye like I should have? Will ye let my granddaughter come and join her rightful family? 'Tis Christmas, after all."

Was he really saying all this? Was she hallucinating? Her eyes burned with tears, and her hands shook. Could she really go back home? No more working as a wet nurse, no more lying, no more loneliness and daily fear for herself and her daughter. Maeve would be safe. Deidre would be home, protected, reunited with her parents, free to do whatever she wanted.

What did she want?

An image of her, Hamish, and Maeve in their own home came to mind. Her putting a delicious stew on the table. Hamish looking at her with longing and heat in his black eyes. Maeve sated, well dressed, and happy, learning to read and write, just like Deidre had.

That was what she wanted. A part of her, anyway. But that was not possible. Hamish was Hamish, and he didn't want to tie himself to anyone, even to his own daughter. As he'd told her, he would support Maeve and her, but he wouldn't commit, he wouldn't risk his heart for them.

But could she believe that her father would truly take her in and never betray her like that again? Working together with Hamish and trusting him to complete his part of the plan had revived her trust. But still...

"How can I be sure ye wilna betray us again, Da? How can I be sure ye'll be true to yer word to protect me and Maeve?"

"I can swear it to ye, lass," he said. "On our blood. I've come to realize honor and pride dinna matter much these days when the English are the overlords. Nothing matters without yer family. Yer kin. And ye're mine. I betrayed ye before, but I will never do that again. I'm getting old, and I dinna have many years left. The thought of that changed my mind like nothing else."

He pulled his dagger out. "I'll prove it. Let me make a blood oath."

Deidre froze, staring at the hand holding the weapon with wide eyes. Her father was ready to do that for her? A blood oath was ancient, deep, and unbreakable. Especially for a man like her father. Tears streamed down her cheeks.

"'Tis nae necessary," she said.

Relief opened her up and all the tension, demons, and fears spilled out of her. She felt light and free, like a bird bathing in the sunlight. Her da opened his arms to her, and she fell into them with a sigh and a happy smile. Through her blurry vision, she saw Hamish watching her with the serene smile of someone who'd accomplished his mission.

She only wished he'd wear that expression after he asked for her forgiveness. After he told her he wanted to spend his life with her.

"Thank ye, Da," she whispered. "I'm so tired of being alone with just Maeve and me against the world. I forgive ye. Ye're right. 'Tis Christmas, and we must put the wrongs of the past behind us. We'll come home with ye."

Deidre would need to tell Lady Matilda she was leaving. She already had a wet nurse in mind who could start right away. She didn't think Lady Matilda would regret Deidre's decision much. The woman only tolerated Deidre. The combination of jealousy, her dislike of Scots, and Deidre's independence would make it easy for Lady Matilda to accept this news.

She let her father go and wiped the tears from her face.

"Ma?" Maeve said behind her back. "What's wrong? Did the man make ye cry?"

Deidre turned to her and smiled. Maeve had her gosling in her hands, and her eyes were wide.

"Nae, my sweet," Deidre said and stretched her arm to Maeve. "Come here. I want ye to meet someone."

Maeve came to her and took her hand as she held the

gosling in the other. "Come meet yer granda," Deidre said, "Chief of clan Maxwell and warden of Scottish West March."

Maeve stared at grandfather, who eyed her with tears in his eyes.

"I have longed to meet ye for years," he said.

"Is he yer da?" Maeve asked Deidre.

"Aye," Deidre said.

"Do I also have a grandma?"

"Aye," said Harris. "And she canna wait to feed ye Christmas dinner."

LATER THAT EVENING, THE GREAT HALL OF CAERLAVEROCK was full of fires and light. Hamish watched Deidre and Maeve at a place of honor at the chief of the clan's table. Maeve sat between her grandfather and her grandmother, both of them cooing over her and asking her questions.

Hamish's heart ached as he watched his daughter's shy but happy grin spread from ear to ear. The gosling, whom Harris bought from the Tailors, ate grain on the table in front of Maeve.

Deidre caught his gaze from across the hall, and he couldn't look away. It felt just like all those years ago, when she was a young lass, and he was a young man who burned for her.

The hall was decorated with holly wreaths, and the leaves reflected the golden light from the fires. Tallow candles stood everywhere. The tables were laden with food and drinks, roasted geese, meat pies, fresh bread, cups with ale, uisge, and wine. The Maxwells must have saved up for the feast, and Hamish knew the members of the clan contributed, too.

A Yule log lay in a brazier in the middle of the great hall, ready to be lit and burned. Never in his life had Hamish had this feeling of belonging and of home. It terrified him how much he liked this. Could he be the lord of his own house one day, just like Harris, with Deidre by his side, and Maeve with them, happy, healthy, and safe?

Did he want that?

More than anything.

But that was like wanting a poisoned pie. It would be delicious and deadly.

Nae. He couldn't. He'd be mad to try. It would be suicide for his heart, because if he allowed himself to be happy and anything happened to Deidre or Maeve, unlike with Fiona, he wouldn't be able to recover.

"Let us burn the Yule log," Harris announced.

Everyone present gathered around the brazier, and Hamish joined the large circle. His adoptive parents in Skye had burned a log every day of the twelve days of Christmas, but it had never felt like this. The four of them—Hamish, Fiona, and their parents had sat around the central hearth of the dirt-poor farmhouse. Their adoptive father had done it like it was another chore.

The eyes of the Maxwell clansmen were lit with wonder.

"Why do we burn the log, Granda?" Maeve said. "We never did it in Carlisle, nae with Innis, and nae with the other families we lived with."

She should be asking her father. Hamish should be the one explaining Scottish traditions. Harris laid his hand on her shoulder. "'Tis to light the night and turn it into day, dove."

He took the torch from his wife's hand and brought it to a sheet of bark set vertically in a slit in the wood. The hall fell silent as the fire licked the kindling and it began to burn. Fire ate through it, soon reaching the bark and spreading to the top of it.

"Let the light guide us through this winter, starting from the day that our Lord Jesus Christ was born."

Hamish looked at Deidre across from the flames, and their gazes locked. He longed to come to her and hug her shoulders, to bring her to him like marrit men hugged their wives. There was a longing in her eyes, too. And heat. And sadness. His chest ached.

When the chunk of wood was burning brightly, some people started to sing, while others went back to their tables to continue eating and drinking.

Deidre took Maeve by the shoulders, and they left the room. She probably wanted to get Maeve to bed. Hamish sat watching the guests eat, feast, and talk, but he didn't really see anyone or anything. Without Deidre, the great hall felt empty, even so full of people. Without her, he didn't know what he was doing here.

He left the hall, too, and climbed down the stairs to get some fresh air in the courtyard. He heard steps on the round landing and looked up. Deidre stood frozen on the stairs. Illuminated by a torch in the sconce behind her, her hair glowed like freshly polished bronze.

She met his gaze. They were alone. Her lips were parted, and the air crackled between them.

"Hamish..."

There she was. Not across the hall. Not behind the walls of Tailor's house. Not somewhere far away, God knew where. He'd longed for her for years. He'd dreamed of her every night. He'd imagined her, fiery and soft and beautiful under him, crying out his name as he brought her higher and higher to the peak of pleasure.

There were no barriers between them now.

He didn't think. He flew up towards her, taking the stairs two at a time. He took her hips in his hands and lifted her up. She gasped, wrapping her arms around his shoulders.

"What are ye—"

"Nae a word, lass." He began climbing the stairs with her still in his arms. "I'm going to take ye to yer bedchamber and make love to ye until ye forget where ye are and what day it is. I havna stopped burning for ye for all these years, and I ken ye want me just as much. I see it in yer eyes. I felt it in our kiss."

They were on the landing of the second floor now. There were three doors and another flight of round stairs leading on the next floor.

"Hamish—"

"I have missed ye. I havna stopped thinking of ye."

I havna stopped loving ye.

She sighed, and her eyes changed, decision burning in blue flames in them. "Take the door to yer right."

CHAPTER 14

Deidre melted like butter under the sun. He kicked the door open with his foot and rushed into her bedchamber with her still in his arms like a caveman.

The feel of him against her, hard and tall and masculine, sent her head spinning and her muscles clenching. He shut the door behind him with another kick. The room was dark, only a fire burned in the fireplace. A canopy bed with draping stood by the opposite wall, and a bearskin lay on the floor as a rug.

She felt like she were flying. Soaring. He'd said he'd missed her, and the truth was she'd missed him, too.

Despite everything that had transpired, she hadn't stopped loving him.

And now that she and her daughter were safely back with her family, more than anything, she wanted to let him make love to her tonight. They just needed to be careful that she didn't get pregnant again.

He wouldn't stay. He wouldn't commit to Maeve and her. Aye, she knew that. There was no way of changing that.

But he wanted her, and she wanted him, and just this once, she'd give in to this fantasy.

He put her feet on the floor and covered her mouth with his. His lips were surprisingly soft. Heat emanated from his body. He smelled like leather and iron and his own, male musk —something dark and crisp, like a night under the stars in a field of clover.

His tongue touched hers, and he tasted delicious. His mouth was hot and sweet. He sucked her tongue gently, and lightning that she'd only felt with him ran through her veins.

She sagged into him, his arms like iron bars around her waist. She rubbed against him like a cat against catnip, and she wasn't even ashamed of herself. He was so hot he incinerated her body even through his tunic.

He let out a low growl in the back of his throat, picked her up, and carried her to the bed. Slowly, he began kissing her chin and down her neck. He ran his hand down her body and found her breast. He cupped it, and Deidre grimaced in discomfort. The last time Stephen had fed was before they left Carlisle when the church bells rang noon.

Her breasts, full of milk, tingled and hurt.

"What is it?" Hamish said.

"Milk," she whispered. "I'm full and aching. There's nae babe to suck on them."

Something dark crossed his face.

"Let me help ye with that."

"What?" She rose on her elbows and watched in fascination as he hooked the hem of her dress and dragged it up and over her body, leaving her only in her smock. He undid the laces of it in the front and revealed one of her breasts.

Deidre watched in fascination as it lay in his hand, creamy white against his tanned, weathered skin.

"So full," he said and looked at her, something like love and wonder and desire in his eyes. "Ye're a woman. Nae the sweet lass I kent all those years ago. Ye're ripe and round and delicious. The fire in ye grew and turned ye core into steel. I dinna think I ken a woman stronger than ye."

Her eyes blurred with tears. His words touched her heart and her soul and washed away all her last reservations like warm water washed dirt. She wasn't even angry at him anymore. He'd saved Maeve and her from the life of a wet nurse at the mercy of complete strangers. Thanks to him, her father was alive, she'd reunited with her clan, and her daughter had a family.

The only thing that saddened her was that they didn't have a future. He didn't love her enough to commit to her and Maeve and risk his heart. But he could give her one night where she pretended that he would.

Her breast ached, and her nipple hardened, a droplet of milk appearing on the tip of it.

Hamish looked at her and lowered his head. He took her nipple in his mouth and sucked. Deidre's head fell back as she arched into his touch, absorbing the beautiful sensation that radiated through her breast. The combination of pleasure and relief drew a low, guttural moan from the back of her throat.

The sensation was wanton. A man sucking on her breasts, drinking her milk, and nae a babe... 'Twas sinful and primal and scorching hot.

Should she even allow him to do this? She didn't want to feel like his mother. And she didn't. Something about this spurred her desire, and she felt wetness gathering at her entrance. She moaned and pressed her thighs together in an attempt to relieve the burning need in her folds.

As though realizing what she wanted, he ran his hand down her thigh, down her knee, and under her smock. She jerked a little at the feel of his callused hand on her inner thigh. As he moved his hand up, she bit her lip.

"Ahhhh," she groaned, and her inner muscles clenched, anticipating Hamish's fingers.

He began sucking the other breast and gently spread the folds of her sex and circled her clit with his thumb. She made an involuntary sound of lust. Her thighs trembled, and her breathing was labored. Pleasure crashed through her core, radiating up her body. He pressed and circled and rubbed, and she clenched, her skin flushed and burning. She was out of her mind and desperate for a release.

It came quickly. Mayhap because of the years of no one touching her this way. Or mayhap his masterful hands still knew her body so well. But one moment she was swimming in a sea of pleasure, and the other, she was convulsing violently, heading into the blinding hot light of the summer sun. She clenched and unclenched as waves of sweet bliss washed through her.

HAMISH WATCHED HIS BONNIE LASS FALL APART UNDER HIS touch. He couldn't remember seeing a more beautiful sight. Her cheeks flushed and her eyes burned. Her full breasts were at his disposal, ripe and heavy and there for the taking.

"Oh, Hamish," she called his name as she undulated against his torso. "Oh, Hamish," she whispered as her body trembled with aftershocks in his arms.

He kissed her misted forehead and stretched on the bed next to her. They'd never made love in a bed before. In hay, in the woods, against the wall of a shed, against a tree, in a river... but never in a bed. It was as though they were home, and she were his wife, and he were her husband. Forever...

He traced her cheek. How soft... She sighed, leaning into his touch, and closed her eyes.

Forever...

Would it be so bad to be with her for the rest of his life? Was the risk so great? Greater than the reward?

It would be a dream.

He kissed her, plunging into the sweet, petal softness of her mouth. She responded, her tongue making leisurely, long strokes against his.

He longed to drive inside of her, to have her hot and sleek and welcoming him. He buried his face in her neck, inhaling the milky, herbal scent of her—sweet and feminine and smoky from the burning log.

"My fiery lass," he said, covering her neck with kisses.

She ran her hands down his tunic and towards his belt. With swift fingers, she undid his belt and tossed it on the floor. It fell with a soft *thud*. She dragged the edge of his tunic up and over his head, and the air felt cool against his heated skin.

Running her fingers down his torso, she traced his battle scars. Every touch of the pads of her fingertips sent a bolt of lightning right into his groin, and his cock swelled more and more.

"Those are new," she whispered. She leaned down and kissed his scars gently. Her lips were featherlight, and every time they connected with his body, his erection jerked.

"Ye ken which ones are new?" he said.

"Oh, aye. I remember every part of yer body. Nae a day passed by that I didna think of ye."

His treacherous heart gave a hard lurch at that. She continued kissing his stomach. "Ye gained weight," she said. "Those muscles like rocks..."

She undid the lace that held his breeches around his waist and pulled them down his hips. His cock jerked next to her face, and she stared at it with the expression of a cat looking at a bowl of cream.

"And I remember this," she said, and a chest-deep growl escaped through his clenched teeth.

"Lass—"

Her lips wrapped around the tip of his cock, and sharp, acute pleasure shot through him. She moved her lips up and down, torturing him. He grunted. How many times had he dreamed of her mouth on him like this? How many times had he pleasured himself while imagining her in this exact position?

No dream could compare to this reality. Her tongue stroked him up and down and around, and soon he couldn't stop from thrusting ever slightly in her mouth with the rhythm of her movements.

And soon, too soon, he was at the verge of spilling. He withdrew quickly. "On yer back, lass. I want to be deep in ye."

She chuckled. "This is one time I'm happy to obey yer command."

He kicked his breeches off and removed her smock. She lay on her back and spread her legs for him. He stood still, frozen, eyeing every inch of her body. She was a strong woman who wasn't opposed to hard work. Her full, round breasts with rosy nipples were perfect. She had a narrow waist and soft stomach, broad, curvy hips, and feminine thighs. And that brown triangle at the apex of them...

He lowered himself on top of her, looking deep into her eyes. "That golden stardust on yer nose, lass—" He kissed her nose and cheeks. "Every time I look at the night sky, I think of ye."

He spread her thighs with his knee and nestled between her legs. He positioned his tip at her entrance and drove into her in one swift motion. She took him in, her body soft and silky smooth and tightening around him. He sank into the blue of her irises like into a deep loch. He felt her muscles clench and tighten around him. She gasped as their connection took them both and wrapped around them like a bubble. He began moving, sliding in and out of her, and intense bliss spread through him with every movement.

She moaned sweet little sounds of pleasure, and he took her into his arms and pressed himself into her, willing for the borders of their bodies to dissolve and for them both to become one.

He flipped them, so that he lay on his back and she straddled him. He intensified his movements, the edge of release chasing him. He pounded into her, the slaps of his body against hers loud in the quiet room. He cupped her breasts and they bounced up and down in his hands, heavy and warm.

She was like a goddess from the sky, beautiful and free, her long hair spilling on her shoulders, her eyes half closed, her lips red. His breathing was ragged, his thighs burned from the motion. And yet nothing was enough. A lifetime of being buried deep within her wouldn't be enough.

Every muscle of his abdomen strained, and he thrust into her in a wild, out-of-control rhythm. She convulsed around his cock with a gasp, and he continued to thrust into her. Her spasms milked him, and she dug her fingernails into his stomach. His own release was about to crest.

"Lass..." he said on a gasp.

Her eyes snapped open in understanding, and she slid off him. He came violently with a groan. He spasmed, and his whole body trembled as he spilled onto her stomach. She collapsed next to him, and he wrapped his arms around her, still jerking with the waves of pleasure that ran through him.

As he stilled and breathed deeply, he kissed her forehead. He wanted this every day of his life. He wanted to have her in his bed and never let her go.

That feeling crashed through his whole body like the rumble of a storm in full swing. The connection they had now was so strong, like they were two entwined branches of the same tree. They had the same roots, one system that connected them.

He'd only ever experienced this feeling of devotion, of being united with someone, with Fiona. When she'd died, it was like his roots had been cut. That was the first day he'd killed someone.

To this day, Bearnas was the only woman he'd ever harmed. She'd deserved it. She was a cruel, selfish, old crone and had taught him a valuable lesson. Not to love again. If he loved someone, he'd be vulnerable to hurt and destruction.

If Deidre and Maeve were taken away from him, it would be worse than losing Fiona. Because not just a part of his soul would die.

The loss would consume him whole.

CHAPTER 15

Deidre swam in a pool of warm, bubbly happiness. She felt heavy and comfortable, as though sunlight was shining on her naked body. She was nestled against Hamish, her face hidden in his neck, his arm around her. She inhaled his masculine scent, feeling loved and cared for and sated.

Though if he wanted to go again, she would be hungry for it. She breathed heavily, enjoying having the man she loved against her.

The man she loved...

He tensed under her cheek, his gaze locked on the ceiling. Deidre bit her lip and traced her finger along his hard, broad chest covered with black hair.

This was happiness. And she wanted more of it. He must feel it, too, this earth-shattering, soul-deep tie that was between them. It hadn't faded with time. It had only grown stronger, especially after what they'd been through.

"What are ye thinking of, Hamish?" she said.

"I'm thinking about leaving."

The words were simple, and yet it felt like a rug had been

pulled from under her feet, and she'd fallen on hard, cold ground, hitting her head and crushing her skull.

"Oh." She sat up and searched for her smock. She shoved it over her head and stood. "Why am I surprised?"

He sat, too, propping himself up with his elbows and eyeing her darkly.

She gestured up and down her body. "Apparently, years pass and I age, but instead of gaining wisdom, I learn nothing."

"Lass, I canna—"

"Ye canna be with anyone. Aye. Ye're a lone wolf. Ye belong with no one. Aye, ye told me, and I heard ye, and yet stupid, silly me still let myself hope. Just like all those years ago, when I was sure that once ye kent about the babe ye'd come to yer senses. But then ye told me ye didna want a family, and I didna want to inflict myself and Maeve on a man who didna want us." She scoffed. "I was so right. Even if I'd told ye about the babe back then, it wouldna have changed anything, aye?"

"It would have changed everything," he barked. He got up and put on his breeches. "But ye're with yer clan now. Yer da's forgiven ye, ye've forgiven him, and he's accepted Maeve. He'll protect ye and provide for ye much better than me. Here ye have the whole clan as yer kin, Deidre. I have no one."

She sighed. "You could have us."

He grasped the edge of the mattress until his knuckles whitened. "'Tis better this way. The lass dinna ken about me. Let's leave it that way."

He put his tunic back on. "Ye dinna want to connect yer life with me. Ye dinna want nae more bairns from me, aye?"

She threw her hands up in the air. "We're nae marrit! And 'tis ye who dinna want anything to do with us."

He grabbed her by the shoulders. His eyes were so intense, they were like claws digging into her skin. There was black despair and a bottomless pain in them. And fear. So much fear in this man who could do anything.

"I want so much more than ye can imagine, Deidre," he

hissed. "Ye dinna ken how much I want it. But I canna put myself at risk of losing ye."

He let her go, and she staggered a little, the floor shifting under her feet.

"Be honest, lass. If I did want to take ye and Maeve, would ye say aye?"

She panted, glaring at him as he waited for her answer.

When she didn't reply, he pressed, "Can ye put everything behind us and trust me?"

Her gut clenched until it spasmed. Aye, it was easy to blame him for everything. But if he did come around and gave her what she thought she wanted, would she be able to open up to him and commit to him? To trust him enough with her heart, and more importantly, with her daughter's heart?

Now that Maeve had found her grandfather and grandmother, that should be enough. He was right, her clan would take care of them and protect them. She didn't need to depend on Hamish.

"I could if I didna have Maeve," she said, her chest growing cold as frost. "But I have Maeve to think of. While I could risk my own heart, I canna risk hers. I canna allow her to love ye and get attached to ye only to be betrayed, rejected, and abandoned in the end."

"I didna abandon her, Deidre. I didna ken of her existence."

"But ye abandoned *me*."

He closed his eyes, as though hit hard by something big and heavy. His nostrils flared as he took a deep breath. He took his belt and his dagger, then wrapped it around his waist.

"So it seems there is no future for us," he said. "Mayhap one day ye'll tell her about me? One day when she's old enough to understand?"

Deidre crossed her arms over her chest. "I dinna think she'll ever understand. But, aye, I will tell her. One day when she wilna get hurt by ye."

He nodded, and the pain in his eyes slit her stomach like a thousand knives. He walked to the door, opened it, and looked over his shoulder. "I will send ye coin. Ye wilna need for anything. Store some away so that she has a good dowry and gets marrit to a good man who will take care of her. Life is harder for a bastart."

CHAPTER 16

Hamish gathered his things and was set to be on his way the very next morning. He couldn't stay here. The very sight of Deidre made him feel like someone had cleaved his chest open and cut out his heart.

He saddled his horse and led out it out of the stables and into the courtyard. The castle was quiet, save for the clanking of dishes and noises from the kitchen.

Hamish put one foot in the stirrup and was about to mount up and ride off, leaving Deidre and Maeve forever. But he couldn't bring himself to. His arms wouldn't pull his body up into the saddle, his leg wouldn't push off the ground.

Just do it...

It was as though invisible hands held him back. He didn't want to leave. He didn't want to go back to his life as a lone wolf.

But what could he do? Where could he go from here? He could go back to Innis and stay with her for a while. Find another job. Go north and negotiate a better price for that island he wanted from the MacDonalds.

Build a house.

Get tenants.

Live alone, always in control of everything. Far away from the two people he longed for the most.

Wind swooshed past him, throwing a handful of prickly snow into his face. That would be his only company on his estate. Wind. Silence. No one to talk to. No one to care for. No heartbreak. No risk. Full control.

"Lord Hamish?" a small voice said behind him.

With his heart aching, he turned around. Maeve stood before him, the gosling chirping in her hands. She wore a woolen cloak with a cape over her head. She stared at him with those big, black eyes.

His eyes.

"Aye, lass?"

"Are ye leaving us?"

"I am."

She pursed her lips in a grimace. "'Tis why Ma is so sad?"

He swallowed. "Is she?"

"Aye. She came to my new bed last night. We're nae used to sleeping apart. I heard her cry."

Hamish was ready to punch himself in the stomach. "Did she say 'twas because of me?"

"Nae."

"Then 'tis probably isna. She probably just missed ye."

"Thank ye for helping my granda find my ma. I still dinna ken why Ma got lost and couldnae find her way back."

'Twas because of me.

"Dinna matter now, birdie. Ye're with family now."

"I only wish my da was here, too."

A sharp pain pierced him right through the middle.

Yer da is here...

"I wish that for ye, too, lass."

He could be. He only needed to say a word. He only needed to let go and allow himself to feel. To take the risk that something might go wrong.

The pain of his heart breaking tore him apart. How awful

was it going to feel being away from Deidre and Maeve, to never see them again? Maybe being with the people he loved was better than isolating himself, even if it brought the potential for pain.

Maybe they could get through whatever life brought together.

Of course, he'd need to convince Deidre she could trust him, that he'd rather cut his own heart out than betray and reject his daughter.

He knew only one way to do that.

"Lass," he said. "Ye should go break yer fast. I'm nae going anywhere. I need to go speak to yer granda first."

DEIDRE STARED AT HER FATHER'S DAGGER IN HER HANDS. SHE was a lady of gentry again. She didn't need to feed a bairn anymore, or wash one, or clean soiled cloths. She didn't need to worry about being paid or finding food her daughter. She didn't need to fear anyone would discover she wasn't a widow, but a fallen woman with a bastart.

She was safe.

She was home.

And she was empty.

Not even empty. This nagging pain in her chest was like five cats scratching at her insides. That wasn't emptiness. It was missing Hamish.

What now? What would her life be like now? She'd have time to teach Maeve to read and write. Mayhap she'd also teach her sword-fighting like her da had taught her. Mother would insist they embroider together, no doubt. They could go falconing. Sew new dresses... And every night, her bed would be empty and cold.

The man she loved would be somewhere far away from her. And she'd live thinking of him every day until the day she died.

Because he was afraid to love, and she was too stubborn to trust him, they would live lives full of regrets. Lonely lives. Empty lives.

Was there really no way for them to reconcile? Could she trust him, fully and irrevocably? Could she really put her heart at risk and teach her daughter to be strong while being vulnerable?

If Hamish had been ready to commit to them, her daughter could've had her father in her life. Life was unpredictable, but Deidre would always be there for her daughter, no matter what.

Warmth spread through her as excitement rushed into her blood. She needed to catch Hamish before he left and see if he would change his mind.

She put the dagger in the belt of her dress and hurried downstairs. When she reached the great hall, she heard Hamish's voice booming from inside. She froze behind the corner to listen.

"I must speak to ye, laird," Hamish said. "Please. Alone."

"Can it wait?" Harris said. "I wanted to show Maeve the falcons."

"It canna wait. And 'tis about Maeve."

"All right. Then whatever ye have to say, say it in front of everyone."

No one spoke for a moment. Deidre's heart drummed in her chest. Was he about to proclaim his fatherhood? Shock washed through her in a cold wave. Her father would kill him.

If he claimed Maeve as his daughter, there would be no going back. Not for Maeve. Not for Hamish. Not for her.

She should go in and stop him.

But she didn't. She waited to hear what he wanted to say. She wanted him to promise in front of everyone that Deidre and Maeve were his. That they all belonged together.

"So?" Harris said.

"I'm here to ask for yer daughter's hand."

Deidre's hand shot to her mouth. The world stilled, and then everything began to move in slow motion.

"What?" he croaked. "What?"

Deidre couldn't wait any longer. She peered out from behind the corner. Her father stood, leaning over the table, staring at Hamish as though he were the devil himself.

"I'm asking for Deidre's hand in marriage," Hamish repeated.

Her heart drummed against her rib cage so hard it might beat its way through.

"Ye? Ye have nae land, nae silver, nothing."

That was not true, but her father didn't know that. "I have Maeve."

Deidre's stomach dropped on the floor. She hurried into the great hall. All faces turned to her. Her mother, the servants, the clansmen and women were all staring in pure astonishment. Her father was livid. Hamish's face lit up like a sunrise when he saw her.

"Hamish..." she said.

"Deidre, what is he talking about?" her father asked.

She came to stand next to Hamish. Their eyes locked, and she finally saw what she'd craved to see ever since they met. There was resolve and unquestionable loyalty to her there.

She took his hand, and they both turned to face her father.

"Hamish is Maeve's father, Da," she said.

"Hamish is my father?" Maeve's voice came from behind them.

Deidre gasped and turned. Maeve stood in the doorway with Maccus in her palms. Deidre's skin misted with sweat. There was no way back now. They were all in.

"Aye, sweet," she said and stretched her hand to her. "He is."

Maeve walked slowly, eyeing them both with her big eyes. "I thought my da was dead."

"I told ye that so ye would nae be hurt, and so that I could find work."

Maeve took her hand and stood eyeing Hamish. He held his breath, his eyes big. And for the first time, Deidre saw fear in them.

"Will ye stay with us then?" Maeve asked. "Or are ye still going to leave—" She bit her lip, then added, "Da?"

Deidre's stomach flipped. Hamish gulped audibly, and his eyes watered.

"I will stay as long as ye'll have me, lass."

She beamed and looked at Deidre. "I'll have him, Ma. Will ye?"

Deidre looked at Hamish, and the last of her reservations washed away. The hard defenses around her heart cracked, and it expanded with pure light. She beamed, taking in his dear face. He grinned back. It was the first time she'd seen such a smile from him.

"Ye asked my da," Deidre said, "and ye asked Maeve if she would have ye. But ye didna ask me."

"I still need to give my consent," Harris grumbled.

"Deidre Maxwell," Hamish said and dropped to one knee. "Will ye be my wife?"

Tears of joy streamed down Deidre's cheeks. Mayhap it was a Christmas miracle that the man she'd loved for years, the father of her child, had come back, saved her from a poor existence, and was finally asking her the question she'd longed to hear.

There was only one thing she could say.

"Aye."

EPILOGUE

Isle of Benfar, Hebrides, six months later...

Hamish split a log with his ax. His muscles sang and burned, his naked torso enjoying the strain of hard work. The Isle of Benfar belonged to him now. Harris Maxwell had given him a small dowry when he marrit Deidre despite Hamish insisting he had enough to provide for them. The work on their new house was in full swing. Masons built the stone walls, carpenters cut and prepared the timber, and his new tenants were building their own houses to the south and north. They'd set up farms and pastures for sheep, since it was important the community could sustain itself on the remote island.

Innis and her two children were among the new settlers. Hamish was glad she'd agreed to move away from her poor life in Carlisle.

On the Isle of Skye, Hamish had heard news of John MacDougall from a merchant from England. John was gravely ill and had fallen out of favor with the king of England. That made Hamish feel safer. Most likely, John had more important things to think about rather than sending assassins after him.

The island was visible from the Isle of Skye in good

weather. It was long and narrow, with a small grove of trees, and rolling hills of heather, moss, and grass. There was a small loch in the middle of the island. The sea breeze was ever present here, cool and strong. But it wasn't a lonely sound anymore. It brought Hamish the sound of hammers, and the noise of men making jests, and the laughter of his daughter.

"Hamish," Deidre said from his right.

Hamish wiped his forehead with the back of his hand and turned to see the most beautiful woman in the world coming towards him with a cup of water in her hands.

"Ah, thank ye, lass." He pulled her close and pressed her against his chest and kissed her. She spilled the water on him and laughed against his mouth.

"Ye're sweaty," she complained.

"Aye," he growled. "Sweaty, dirty, and burning for ye."

He bit her lip playfully, and she gave in to the kiss, sagging against him, and boiling the blood in his veins. He felt her breasts pressed against his torso, and her belly, swollen with their second child, nudged at his stomach.

When they were both breathless, and he was ready to tear her dress off her, he leaned back and said, "Ye ken it only means I'll need to go and bathe ye in the loch. I dinna mind."

She laughed, and he couldn't hide his smile. She got that look on her face, the look of wonder that he'd never truly deserve but accepted like he accepted everything from her. She touched his lips.

"God, I love it when ye smile, Hamish," she said and pecked his lips with hers. "If I can put a smile on yer face every day..."

"Ye do."

She nuzzled his neck. "Anyway, I came to call ye for midday meal. The stew is ready."

He wiped his hands and put on his tunic. "Aye. Let's go eat."

They sat around a small campfire next to the tent where

they'd slept ever since they'd arrived on the island two moons ago. Maeve joined them, and Maccus, who'd turned out to be a female goose, grazed three feet away from a faerie ring of white mushrooms nearby. Hamish looked at the circle and thought of that meal he'd shared with the copper-haired woman, Sìneag, who'd told him how George Tailor might have a job for him, and how he might find true love there. Looking at Deidre and Maeve, Hamish thought that Sìneag had been exactly right.

Maccus honked and wobbled closer to a bigger male goose who grazed by Maeve's side. Maeve called him Stephen, to remind herself of the wee bairn in Carlisle she'd loved. There hadn't been any goslings yet, but Maeve was looking forward to starting a goose colony in her new home.

The wee cauldron smelled of fish stew. Maeve sat by Hamish's side and leaned tenderly against his arm. He hugged his daughter and kissed the top of her head, briefly inhaling the sweet scent of her. Wind played with her black hair, and she tucked a strand behind her ear. He studied the brown stardust on her nose and cheeks, which had grown darker and expanded during spring and summer.

They ate the stew, exchanging jests and listening to Maeve telling them what she'd done that day.

"'Tis so green here," Maeve said, looking around, "And so... mysterious. I dinna ken why, but I almost believe in faeries here. 'Tis different than down in Carlisle."

Deidre chuckled. "Ye're half Highlander, lass. Mayhap yer da has a story or two to tell?"

Hamish looked around. "Aye. I do. I dinna remember my real ma much, but I do remember Bearnas, my adoptive mother, telling stories of fairies. She wasna a good woman, but some of her stories were good. There was one about a faerie who looks to create happiness for people through time. If ye're a good person, and there's a soul mate for ye, even if that person is born many years in the past or many years in the future, she'll send ye through time to yer soul mate."

Maeve's eyes filled with wonder. "Oh, aye? I've never heard of a faerie like that."

Hamish chuckled. "Aye, well, nae many ken it. 'Tis an interesting story. I did meet a woman once who told me she was a time traveler. I didna believe her, of course."

"Ye didna believe her?" Maeve said.

"Nae, lass. I've seen enough in the world to ken that nae miracles exist—except ye and yer ma. And yer future brother or sister."

"Where did ye meet the woman who said she was a time traveler, Da?"

"'Twas in Inverlochy Castle, a couple of years ago."

"A castle? Like Granda's castle? What did ye do there?"

"I was working for the MacDougall clan, looking for a secret tunnel to help them take the castle. The constable of the castle, Craig Cambel, marrit the lass thinking she were the daughter of the chief MacDougall, but in the end, she'd claimed she was a time traveler."

"Did she go back to her time?" Maeve said. "Or did she stay with him?"

He chuckled. "I dinna ken what happened to her. Mayhap the story is true. After all, I got a true miracle in my life. Ye."

She sighed, looking at the sea dreamily. "I'd like to see another time, though 'tis scary."

Hamish hugged her. "I wilna let ye go anywhere, and when the time comes for lads to seek yer hand, I will deny every single one, because ye're my treasure." He kissed her forehead, and she giggled.

"He doesna mean that, sweet," Deidre said. "If ye love someone, he'll let ye marry him. If 'tis a good man, of course."

Later, when darkness descended on the island and work was halted for the night, Hamish and Deidre walked towards the shore and stood listening to the waves crashing against the cliffs. The sound was lulling, and beautiful, and felt like home.

Stars were shining, the moon was bright, and the summer evening was cool. It smelled like sea and heather, and when he brought Deidre towards him and buried his nose in her hair, she smelled of midnight wonder.

"Mayhap ye're a faerie, Deidre," he said, studying her face lit with the light of countless stars and the moon. "Ye bewitched me with one glance."

She laughed. "Mayhap. I certainly bewitched ye enough for ye to let go of yer wolfish independence."

He kissed her nose and her cheeks. "'Twas yer golden stardust. The shadows of the stars on yer skin."

She laughed. "Mayhap. But I'm still waiting for ye to say the three words that ye've never said to me."

He turned her to face him. His heart was so full, it felt like his chest was about to burst open. Her icy-blue eyes were indigo now, and sparkling brighter than those stars.

He knew what she meant. Although they were marrit now, and he'd loved her for many years, he'd never said that to her. Not even on their wedding day or their wedding night. It wasn't that he didn't want to say it. It was just that he loved her so much, every time he wanted to say it, his muscles seized with emotion and choked him.

He wanted to tell her. He wanted to scream it to the world. She was his, and he was hers.

"I love ye," he said, his throat tightening. Her eyes watered.

"And I love ye, Hamish. Ye the love of my life. The big bad wolf who stole my heart and gave me the greatest gift."

"And yet ye've given me so much more, lass. Last Christmas, ye gave me everything."

THE END

Enjoyed the story? It's the part of my Scottish, time travel series "Called by a Highlander" where strong men and women travel back in time.

If you enjoy time travel romance, read Highlander's Captive, Book One, where you see Hamish in a different role and meet warriors of clan Cambel as they fight in the Wars of Scottish Independence alongside Robert the Bruce. All the while strong modern people navigate through the world of Middle Ages and fight for love.

ALSO BY MARIAH STONE

CALLED BY A HIGHLANDER SERIES (TIME TRAVEL):

Sìneag (FREE short story)

Highlander's Captive

Highlander's Hope

Highlander's Heart

Highlander's Love

Highlander's Christmas (novella)

Highlander's Desire

Highlander's Vow (release 2021)

Highlander's Bride (release 2021)

More instalments coming in 2021 and 2022

CALLED BY A VIKING SERIES (TIME TRAVEL):

One Night with a Viking (prequel)—grab for free!

The Fortress of Time

The Jewel of Time

The Marriage of Time

The Surf of Time

The Tree of Time

CALLED BY A PIRATE SERIES (TIME TRAVEL):

Pirate's Treasure

Pirate's Pleasure

A CHRISTMAS REGENCY ROMANCE:

The Russian Prince's Bride

ENJOY THE BOOK? YOU CAN MAKE A DIFFERENCE!

Please, leave your honest review for the book.
As much as I'd love to, I don't have financial capacity like New York publishers to run ads in the newspaper or put posters in subway.

But I have something much, much more powerful!

Committed and loyal readers

If you enjoyed the book, I'd be so grateful if you could spend five minutes leaving a review on the book's Amazon page.

Thank you very much!

JOIN THE ROMANCE TIME-TRAVELERS' CLUB!

Join the mailing list on mariahstone.com to receive exclusive bonuses, author insights, release announcements, giveaways and the insider scoop of books on sale - and more!

Join Mariah Stone's exclusive Facebook author group to get early snippets of books, exclusive giveaways and to interact with the author directly.

SCOTTISH SLANG

aye – yes

bairn - baby

bastart - bastard

bonnie - pretty, beautiful.

canna- can not

couldna – couldn’t

didna- didn't ("Ah didna do that!")

dinna- don't ("Dinna do that!")

doesna – doesn’t

fash - fuss, worry ("Dinna fash yerself.")

feck - fuck

hasna – has not

havna - have not

hadna – had not

innit? - Isn't it?

isna- Is not

ken - to know

kent - knew

lad - boy

lass - girl

marrit – married

nae – no or not
shite - faeces
the morn - tomorrow
the morn's morn - tomorrow morning
uisge-beatha (uisge for short) – Scottish Gaelic for water or life / aquavitae, the distilled drink, predecessor of whiskey
verra – very
wasna - was not
wee - small
wilna - will not
wouldna - would not
ye - you
yer – your (also yerself)

ABOUT THE AUTHOR

When time travel romance writer Mariah Stone isn't busy writing strong modern women falling back through time into the arms of hot Vikings, Highlanders, and pirates, she chases after her toddler and spends romantic nights on North Sea with her husband.

Mariah speaks six languages, loves Outlander, sushi and Thai food, and runs a local writer's group. Subscribe to Mariah's newsletter for a free time travel book today!

facebook.com/mariahstoneauthor
instagram.com/mariahstoneauthor
bookbub.com/authors/mariah-stone
pinterest.com/mariahstoneauthor

Printed in Great Britain
by Amazon

66643531R00083